YOU'RE IT

A FORBIDDEN, DAD'S BEST FRIEND, LASER TAG ROMANCE

CLEO WHITE

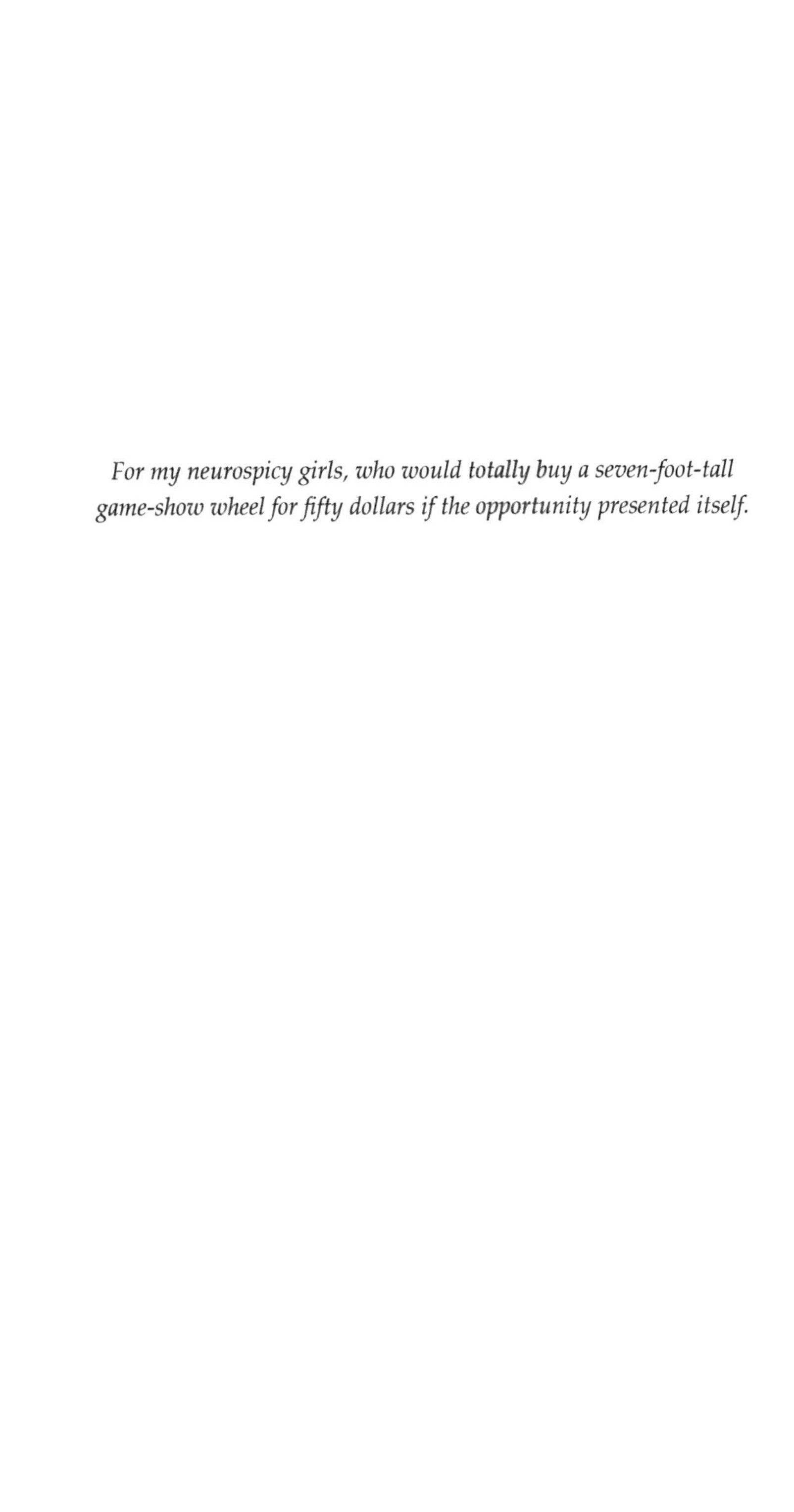

For my neurospicy girls, who would totally buy a seven-foot-tall game-show wheel for fifty dollars if the opportunity presented itself.

To Do: ☆

Find a realtor for GG

Meeting with accountant

Find an accountant

CHAPTER 1
SAVVY

N TWENTY-SEVEN YEARS of extremely questionable decision-making, entering this bathroom may be the dumbest thing I've ever done.

All the signs were there: the dry-heave-worthy smell, the flickering fluorescent lights, the fact that the tiles are brown when I know they used to be blue... All signs pointed to a truly dreadful pee-elimination experience. If I had any other choice *at all*, I would have turned around and driven down the street to the nearest fast-food place.

Unfortunately, the mocha latte I drank on the way here is ready to make me wet myself for the first time since I was six —okay, *eight*—and the time for such luxury has come and gone. Drastic measures need to be taken, and in this case, that means braving the *Texas Chainsaw Massacre* of bathrooms.

"Have fun," Raven calls after me, exuding a level of mocking amusement that only a lifelong best friend can get away with. She'd peeked into the bathroom too and decided she could wait to release her three sips of water in the wild.

Lucky bitch.

"*Ew, ew, ew.*" I edge inside, taking care to avoid the puddle of something that's settled on the grimy floor.

How the hell did it get this bad? The last time I visited Dad at work, maybe a year ago, Galactic Guild had been the same as it always was. Sure, the neon sign out front hadn't lit up in the better part of a decade and the snack bar boasted a health hazard or two, but even that wasn't unusual. There was still a birthday party running around screaming in the arena, a DnD campaign hunched over the table in the back room, and a handful of teenagers in the arcade trying to pretend they were too cool for Dance Dance Revolution.

My eyes burn as I step over what appears to be a desiccated hotdog. Everything was *normal*, damn it. Dad was his usual cheerful but distracted self, the business was busy but run-down, and I told him I was happy but lied. Was that the last ordinary day we spent together before—*nope*. Not going there. I know emotional quicksand when I see it, and I don't have time for that kind of self-sabotage right now.

Being careful to breathe through my mouth, I pause, staring helplessly at the lone corner stall. The rusty metal door is closed, but if the inside is anything like the rest of this bathroom, I'm going to need a shower, and possibly a hepatitis shot, once this is over. Still, my bladder is pleading for relief. If I so much as sneeze right now, it's game over, and I know what needs to be done.

Summoning my courage, I nudge the bottom of the door with my boot, and—*Instant regret.*

Somehow, the small space is even more appalling than the rest of the bathroom.

I'm not sure where to look first. At the giant, crusty poop jutting triumphantly from a few inches of murky water, at the toilet paper hanging over the rim, or the dirty plunger stuck to the ceiling. I settle on gazing, in muted disbelief and horror, at the words graffitied on the wall above the whole shit show.

Caleb's CaCa Lies Here is written in black marker and accompanied by an arrow, directing my attention back to the writer's dubious creation.

My head drops to the side, morbid curiosity delaying my inevitable vomit and/or pants peeing. Without thinking, I step away, and the heel of my sneaker comes down on something crusty. Oh god. *The hotdog.* My stomach rolls and— Okay. I'm done.

Not waiting around for a football-sized rat, supervillain, or zombie to appear from the shadows of this godforsaken wasteland, I book it.

Raven is where I left her, leaning against the opposite wall, and cackles when I vault back through the door. "That bad?"

"Worse," I whine, looking around frantically, as though a usable toilet is going to appear out of nowhere. "And Caleb really needs to seek professional help. There's no way he's getting even close to enough fiber in his diet."

"Who's Caleb?"

"No idea."

Raven looks back toward the bathroom, confusion written all over her face. "Can't you just… hover over it?"

I scoff, gesturing helplessly to my lower half. "No! Look at these things!" My legs are pretty decent, or so I've always thought. They're strong, curvy, and don't regrow waxed hair too fast. What they are not, however, is long enough to hover over whatever viral plague is replicating on that toilet seat. Raven, with her tall-girl privilege, couldn't imagine.

Without another word, I dart off toward the lobby and shove open the grimy glass door. Galactic Guild occupies three quarters of an aging strip mall, located just a little too far from town to attract much foot traffic. The only other business in sight, an after-school karate place, is closed.

There's only one option left.

Trying to run with your thighs pressed together is easier said than done, but I manage a kind of rapid waddle around the back of the building. There's only forest back here, and I hardly bother to confirm I'm alone before scurrying down the embankment and ripping my pants down.

Tree bark cutting into my back is a fair sacrifice for the relief I feel as my pee hits the forest floor.

Holy crap. That was awful.

A crunching of pine needles makes my heart stall, but as I turn toward the hill, I see it's only Raven with a stack of napkins in hand. "You've been shamed enough, so I won't even hold these hostage until you agree to go to that slam poetry night with me. I'm a good friend like that."

I groan in thanks. "You're so nice to me."

"I know. I've grown fond of this nonsense." She turns away with a long sigh, allowing me the opportunity to pull my pants up without an audience. "So, if Stone weren't dead, I'd be pretty pissed at him for leaving you with this mess."

"This mess" being my inheritance of a failing laser tag arena, a pile of medical bills, and a house he mortgaged into the stratosphere to keep said business afloat. In Dad's defense, he hadn't expected to be dead at forty- five. I'm sure he thought he had time, that he could work his way out of the hole and make Galactic Guild as successful as it was decades ago. Unfortunately, having more time isn't a right, and now the asshole gets to float through the afterlife scot-free while I struggle under the burden of his poor decisions.

I make too many of those on my own to be saddled with anyone else's, thank you very much.

"Come on." I kick some leaves over the dirty napkins. "The realtor will be here soon."

Sure enough, when Raven and I round the building, a shiny white sports car is parked beside my beat-up sedan. Its owner, a middle-aged Black woman who looks like she's never had a bad hair day in her life, is stepping out onto the cracked asphalt.

"Hi, Amy?" I approach, smiling brightly, as though her

impression of me will change the market value of my shitty inheritance.

Amy shakes my hand confidently, her eyes already tracking over the weeds poking out of the sidewalk and the broken pinball machine stationed beside the front door. "Good to meet you, Sally."

"It's Savvy, actually," I correct, trying not to grimace.

No one in the history of anywhere has been as poorly named as me. It was pretty optimistic of my parents to give it to me, considering neither of them were ever particularly functional adults and had no business bringing another human being into the world. In a predictable but cruel twist of fate, I am probably the least savvy Savvy that's ever lived.

Not like Amy; she would have been a good Savvy, I can tell.

"Of course. I apologize, I had terrible service when we spoke on the phone," she says smoothly, offering Raven a polite smile before returning to her examination of the building. "You inherited this property recently?"

"I—yeah. My father's owned it since I was very young, but he passed away a few weeks ago."

"I'm very sorry to hear that." She adjusts the strap of her expensive-looking bag, frowning. "Listen, I won't mince words here. The listing price you mentioned isn't realistic. You're about five miles past city limits, and it's not retail friendly. Have there been any updates?"

"Updates?"

"The roof, electrical system?" she suggests, raising her eyebrows, and I want to shrivel up and die on the spot.

Raven—bless her—saves me from responding. "Nope. No updates. Stone wasn't big on capital improvement. He was a firm believer in letting everything go to hell, then patching it up with some duct tape."

Amy's lack of reaction to this is a testament of her professionalism. "I see."

"Listen," I plead, clamping down on the tightening in my chest, which promises a full-blown breakdown is imminent. "I just need to break even. I'm seriously not looking to make a profit or anything, I just want to get rid of this place and pay off the debt. What would it sell for? Realistically."

The obviously savvy Amy produces a sheet of paper and hands it to me. The handwritten number she's circled at the top makes my stomach plummet right through the cracked asphalt. "Commercial space isn't in demand at the moment, and less ideal properties will sit on the market for a while," she explains, glancing back at the strip mall with a sympathetic look.

Oh god.

Sensing the spiral is nearly upon us, Raven loops her arm through mine and asks confidently, "What would you recommend?"

Amy doesn't miss a beat. "Get the business up and running." She nods toward the burnt-out neon lettering that spells out *Galactic Guild Arena* in a bold, futuristic script. "It would be a lot easier to sell a profitable, operational business than the building. Then, once you get the other owner on board—"

I choke. "Excuse me? Other owner?"

"I checked the city's database when I got your call." She produces another document. "It's possible there was some kind of recording error."

There wasn't.

I know it as soon as I read the first line, which heads up a very official, legal-looking deed of sale. Galactic Guild Arena's money troubles weren't new. Apparently, Dad had been bailing the place out for far longer than I knew, going so far as to sell off half the business to—

"I'm going to use Stone's ashes in Arnold's litter box," Raven hisses savagely, her grip on my arm tightening.

Someone is making a weird, hysterical laughing noise

now, but it isn't coming from either of the other women I'm standing with. It's only after I look around wildly, searching for the source, that I realize it's me.

Oh good, mental spiral engaged, right on schedule.

While normally I'd be pretty embarrassed to be full-on losing it in front of a stranger who so clearly has her crap together, I'm so far past caring at the moment. What's worse than inheriting one failing business and a worthless property? When it turns out that you only own half of it, and your dad sold the other half to a man you were hoping never to see again.

"We'll, uh, call you!" Raven assures Amy, steering me back toward the door of Galactic Guild.

"Oh my god, I can't believe this is happening." I gasp through peals of laughter as we enter the darkened lobby, using my sleeve to wipe my eyes.

Raven is muttering under her breath as she deposits me in one of the snack-bar chairs. "I'm going to slap you if you don't stop making that noise," she warns, but despite knowing from experience that this is not an idle threat, I'm helpless.

The hollow, conflicted grief that I've felt since Dad passed is sharper now, more bitter, because how could he have done this? How could he have poured every single penny he had, and plenty of other people's too, into something that was objectively a failure?

Stone Laurence ruined himself, died, and now it's on me to clean up the mess?

Me, who thought it was a good idea to let my college roommate pierce my nipples because her cousin was apprenticing at a tattoo shop, and *"she totally told me what to do".*

Me, who decided a company called Nice n' Cheap Protection was a legitimate source for car insurance.

Me, who has failed or quit every single thing I've ever started.

I've been a legal adult for under a decade, and already, life has chewed me up and spit me back out. I doubt there's anyone *less* qualified to work their way out of a shit show of this magnitude than I am.

Unfortunately, it seems like I don't have a choice.

"You could reject the inheritance?" Raven suggests feebly, as my ridiculous laughter dies away and the unnatural stillness of this place presses in on me. "That's a thing, right?"

It is a thing; I looked it up. However, in yet another testament to my un- savviness, it's too late for that. "I used his life insurance to pay some bills," I confess, staring at the faded purple carpet, hollowed out and numb with disbelief. "This place is mine, whether I want it or not."

Not just mine, though. Nope. And it's saying a lot that in a morning full of unpleasant surprises, finding out who owns the other half of Galactic Guild is worse than even Caleb's caca.

CHAPTER 2
DARWIN

THE TROUBLE WITH DREAMS is they take up a lot of space.

You spend years of your life working, striving, and bettering yourself, for one singular purpose. It's all you think about, all you *want* to think about, and the only thing that matters. Everything else comes second.

You don't make friends, because you're too busy. You don't start a family, because it would be selfish.

You don't find hobbies, because they would occupy time that should be used for *the dream*.

And you never stop to consider what will happen if you make it to the finish line. It never occurs to you that the weight of all those sacrifices might suddenly fall squarely on your shoulders, taking up all the room in your mind that was once occupied by the very dreams that created it.

The irony isn't lost on me.

Things were good when I was working. My compulsions were manageable. There were entire days, weeks even, when I felt like I was in control of my mind. No gnawing fear, no sick twists of shame, or hands that went raw from too much washing.

I was normal, or at least as close to normal as I've ever been. Even with healthy coping mechanisms for my brain's more frustrating idiosyncrasies, I was still an antisocial borderline-recluse with control issues and—as my agent has declared on more than one occasion—a stick up my ass.

Stone's was the only company I actually enjoyed, apart from my own.

My friend was content to take me as I was, never asking for more than I could give, and never offering up more of himself than I wanted. He seemed to have a sixth sense about when I found myself becoming isolated or lonely, and would appear at my door with a six-pack of beers, a new video game, and all the enthusiasm he had when we were fourteen.

It's been almost a month since he died, and in that time, things have begun... slipping.

I have begun slipping.

Maybe I'd have been able to get through it with my sanity intact if it was only losing Stone. That wasn't all, though. No. In a poetic twist of fate, the final book in the series—the dream which miraculously came to fruition and dominated my entire adult life—was published only a week before I got the news that my friend was gone.

It wasn't a surprise. I'd known he was going to die, had known the moment he told me about his diagnosis that I'd soon have to face a world without Stone Laurence.

Receiving adequate warning didn't make the blow any less devastating.

Foolishly, I thought I would be okay. After all, I spent most of my time alone, and preferred it that way. I hadn't accounted for reaching the end of the story I'd dedicated my life to telling, and acknowledging it had filled a much larger place inside me than I realized.

Stone was gone, my dream achieved, and whatever shaky foundation I built my mental health upon has been falling away, bit by bit, ever since.

The fact I'm standing in the middle of my kitchen on a Tuesday afternoon, holding a sledgehammer and staring at the basement door, is obviously a sign that the last piece has finally crumbled to dust.

I doubt many stable, fully functioning adults are so bothered by their home gym smelling like sweat that they decide demolishing the drywall is a reasonable solution. It's *not* reasonable. I know it isn't. The room has probably smelled the same for years, and I had no trouble dismissing it as a moderately unpleasant fact of life.

Unfortunately, knowing something objectively isn't enough to stop it from bothering me. For weeks, The Smell has felt as real as I am. It crawled beneath my skin, buried into my subconscious, and all attempts to resist ended the same way: with me staring at that door, furious with myself.

I was determined today would be different.

Even with the last of the books complete and no new writing prospects, I still had work to do. Years ago, a major television company purchased the option to adapt the series, and filming is now about to begin. It's a valuable opportunity, and one I should take advantage of, regardless of the questionable state of my mental health. There are requests for interviews, requests for comments, requests for me to review other books. There's more than enough to occupy my time, and all of it's more productive than scrubbing every inch of my basement for the third time in three days.

That door in the corner of the kitchen had become my personal Pandora's box, and as long as I didn't look at it, I would be fine.

Things began promisingly. I made my coffee, careful to keep my eyes on the task at hand. While waiting for the pot to brew, I read an article on my phone about olfactory hallucinations and left a bad rating for the grocery store, who delivered my order with non-organic hummus. The Smell was there, like a shadow lingering behind my more ordinary thoughts, but I didn't acknowledge it.

I was pleased with myself.

But, as I went to retrieve my favorite mug, I made a critical error. I failed to account for the glass on the kitchen cabinet. Glass that, regrettably, reflects *the door*.

Gritting my teeth, I stared at it, willing myself not to move.

What did it matter if the basement smelled like sweat? It's a *gym*, for fuck's sake, and now that Stone is dead, the only people who ever visit me at home are my agent, my publicist, and my PA. All of who only show up when absolutely necessary and know better than to venture past the office. The Smell isn't likely to be noticed by anyone but me, and it's ridiculous to be affected so strongly by my own body odor.

It doesn't matter.

The sick, twisted feeling in the pit of my stomach, the one that already knew what had to happen, said otherwise. It *did* matter. The Smell had won; I had lost.

Funnily enough, total annihilation hadn't even been on the table before this. There were other, more reasonable, measures to be taken. Painting was an option, or replacing the floors. I hadn't tried either, but had run through three bottles of bleach, thrown out the curtains, and put all the exercise equipment on the back patio.

When I stormed into the garage in search of medical-grade disinfectant, my gaze caught on the steel-topped tool instead. There it was, hanging innocently on the wall, and it occurred to me that demolishing the walls might be a more appropriate course of action.

The Smell has to be in the drywall.

Ergo, if I get rid of the drywall, The Smell will be gone. If The Smell is gone, I'll be fine.

I'm just reentering the kitchen, filled with a vicious satisfaction at the prospect of ending this for good, when the sound of the doorbell makes me freeze. I glance down at the sledgehammer, then toward the entryway, distracted because *who the hell would be here?*

Curiosity temporarily pulling me from my path of destruction, I set the tool on the kitchen counter and stride through the house just as another chime cuts the silence.

For fuck's sake, did they think pressing it a second time would make a difference? Either I'm home or I'm not.

Irritated beyond belief, I wrench the door open and glower down at the pink-haired woman who's already turned back toward the aging sedan in the driveway. "Can I help you?" I snap, not bothering to disguise my impatience. She came to my home uninvited and interrupted me. Why should I be polite?

The woman's shoulders stiffen and, for a moment, I think she's going to keep walking.

I've opened my mouth to make some harsh comment about her wasting my time, but then she turns around and something deep inside me pulls taut.

"Savvy."

Though I know her instantly, the sound of her name on my tongue feels wrong. The last time I laid eyes on this woman, she was eighteen and little more than a child. Even then, she'd been a force of nature: beautiful, intelligent, and *wild*. I'd felt unsettled by her, a light wind disrupting the waters of my obsessively orderly life. Now...

Now, instinct tells me that Savvy Laurence is no light wind; she's a tornado.

"Hi, Dar." The corners of her lips lift in a tight smile.

Dar.

Savvy's the only one who's ever called me that, apart from family members, and my frosty relationship with them means I haven't heard it in years. Not since the last time she walked out of this house—since I *sent her* out of this house.

It seems to take much more effort to swallow than it ordinarily would because—*fuck me*—she's changed. Stone's little girl isn't a girl anymore, and the beauty of the woman on my doorstep is impossible. Her face has lost its roundness, her body is fuller in certain places and narrower in others and, fuck, were her eyes always that big?

For the first time in recent memory, I don't have a scathing retort on the tip of my tongue. Hell, at this point, I would settle for the ability to speak, but that's gone too.

She's astonishing.

We stare at each other, respective memories of our last interaction hanging in the air between us. Stronger than ever before, regret twists bitterly inside me.

"It's good to see you." Casual. Good. Yes. What happened was a long time ago, she was young… I've done my best not to think about it, and she's probably written the whole thing off as an embarrassing, youthful mistake.

I refuse to examine why that suddenly bothers me.

Her eyebrows pull together, apprehension playing out right across her face. I'd forgotten about that, how expressive she always was. Stone used to call her his open book.

At the thought of my friend, a fresh wave of guilt crashes over me, so heavy it's suffocating. Savvy might be a grown woman, but she's Stone's daughter, his only child, and here I am looking at her like—well, like I'm allowed to look at her at all.

"I'm sorry to come here like this." Her voice is casual, even friendly, but I don't miss the way her hand tightens on the strap of her bag. "Do you have a minute to talk?"

Savvy doesn't need to be shown where to go. In nine years, the house hasn't changed, and she slips past me, careful not to catch my eye, and heads right for the kitchen.

Blowing out a shaky breath, I pause to compose myself before following.

The room is somehow smaller with Savvy seated at one of the island stools, shoulders stiff and eyes glued to a spot over my left ear. There was a time when she'd sat in that same place, her feet on the counter and a bowl of popcorn in her lap, quizzing me about my current work in progress.

I knew how to make her laugh.

"How are you?" I ask, because it seems like the correct thing to say to your late friend's daughter.

Her hands fold neatly on the counter. "Good. And you?"

Suddenly conscious of my own, I shove them into my front pockets. "Good."

"I heard about the show. Congratulations."

"Thank you."

We're being painfully formal. Ordinarily, I have no problem with letting people linger in awkward, stilted silence, but as Savvy's eyes fall to the sledgehammer still sitting where I left it, I ache to fill the chasm between us.

Putting people at ease isn't something I have much experience in, but before I can even make an attempt, Savvy seems to summon her courage. "Dad owed you money."

I hesitate, trying to wade through my disjointed thoughts. "Yes. He did." I'd never hesitated to lend Stone money, although I probably should have. My oldest friend wasn't an especially adept businessman, but Stone and Galactic Guild had been there for me when making a living as an author was still a far-fetched dream.

I worked there just after he bought the place with an inheritance from his parents.

At the time, Stone was newly married to his high school girlfriend, and she was pregnant with Savvy. Meanwhile, I was sinking further away from reality, losing myself in my own imagination and growing increasingly obsessed with the story I was trying to tell. My obsessive tendencies were escalating, beginning to affect my behavior and not just my thinking.

I wasn't a good employee. My disorder wasn't as debilitating as it would be later—before I got a diagnosis, medication, and therapy—but it was still there. Not many people are looking to hire an eighteen-year-old high school dropout who would ignore customers to write nonsensical notes to himself or spray down their workspace with disinfectant precisely six times every thirty minutes.

My family had written me off, but not Stone. My friend believed in me, *accepted me,* and I wrote my first bestseller in between handing out prizes at the arcade ticket counter. How was I supposed to turn my back on him when I could afford to help?

Then there was Savvy, the closest thing I had to a niece, who depended on her father's business.

Savvy, who was bright and bold and deserved the entire world.

Savvy, who I couldn't let suffer for Stone's mistakes.

Savvy, who sits in front of me now, a stranger.

Her eyes lift to the ceiling, as though she's trying to keep herself from crying.

"The agreement was between me and Stone. I don't expect you to pay his debts," I assure her, hating that she expected I'd hold her to it.

After an age, warm, caramel eyes lower to meet mine. "You bought half the business."

I stare. "Are you selling?"

"No. *I can't.*" Her voice cracks, desperation beginning to bleed through the carefully composed, stoic facade. "The market is bad, and the building is too far out of town to be desirable. It needs upgrades. There's… debt." She shakes her head miserably. "It's a mess. Stone was an idiot. Basically, our choices are fixing everything up and making Galactic Guild profitable or losing a lot of money."

"I see."

She blows out a long breath, and I can tell she's trying to pull herself back together. "You're the last person I want to be asking for money from. You've done enough for Dad over the years, but we're both in this mess he made, and"—her bottom lip trembles—"I can't afford to do all the repairs and everything on my own. There's no way."

Reaching into her purse, she pulls out a folded piece of paper and slides it over the counter to me.

I want to read it. I *should* read it. There's nothing stopping me from reaching out and picking it up. Except the memory of her bare fingers touching the paper, and the clawing weight of fear that comes with it.

Motionless, I stare down at the paper, willing myself to *just fucking pick it up*. Seconds tick by. It's my second self-imposed test of the day, and now, I know it will be the second failure too.

I'm in no condition to help anyone.

The sensible thing to do would be to cut my losses now and walk away without wasting another penny on my late friend's behalf. I don't owe Savvy anything. We haven't spoken in nearly a decade, and god knows we didn't part on good terms.

Objectively, I should turn her away.

Objectivity is apparently not on the menu for tonight, because as silence stretches between us, I realize I don't care about what I do or don't owe Savvy. I care about the worried, exhausted look on her face, and struggling under the urge to fix every last problem in her life so she never feels this way again. It's an obsession. I'm familiar with those, as they've dominated my entire life, but this one is different.

Taking care of her isn't something I want to resist.

Without another word, I reach into my back pocket and pull out my wallet. "Here." I take out my credit card, the one with an ungodly high limit that I rarely use, and slide it over the marble counter toward her. "Do whatever you need to."

Savvy blinks at me, looking disoriented by this turn of events. "*That's it?*"

"Did you want me to argue with you? The situation seems fairly straightforward."

Savvy scoffs, leaning back in her chair. "I don't have any management experience. Emptying the quarters out of the pinball machines for Dad was about all I learned how to do. What makes me qualified to do all this?"

I tilt my head to the side, studying her. "Should I say no?" Her mouth pops open in horror. "Of course not!"

A lock of pink hair has fallen over her face, and I imagine what it would be like to reach out and tuck it back behind her ear.

What the hell is wrong with me?

Shoving away the dangerous thought, I force a tight smile. "Well, then, you're in luck. You're intelligent, Savvy. I have no doubt you'll figure everything out."

Her gaze falls to where I'm gripping the edge of the countertop, and I see her eyes widen in horror. A moment too late, I realize what she's looking at.

My hands.

Hands that are scrubbed raw and cracked from the number of times I've washed them over the last few weeks.

I shove them in my pockets, but it doesn't matter. She's seen.

Tense silence falls between us as shame crawls up my body. "I'm sorry to show up like this." There's no mistaking the bitterness or hurt in her voice, and a whole new chasm of regret cracks open inside me.

"I'm glad you came." It's the truth, but Savvy's expression doesn't change. She doesn't believe me. Why would she? Time is supposed to heal all wounds, but this one was never allowed to. I sent her away, and, just as I asked, she never came back.

Until now.

I hid from the damage, buried it, and now it's reemerging, fresh and bitter and terrible as ever.

How could I not have tried to fix our relationship in all that time?

How could I have said those things in the first place?

"I should go," Savvy says, already getting to her feet. All I can do is watch mutely as she slips the credit card into her bag, carefully avoiding my eyes. "I'll send you an email with weekly updates."

I nod, trying to ignore the dangerous tugging in the center of my chest as the sun from the kitchen window catches in her bright hair. "Sounds good."

Should I apologize and try to ease some of the tension between us, or let things stand as they have? Seeing her shouldn't change a thing, but it has.

I don't want her to go.

The quiet and stillness I've always craved, the comfort of my carefully controlled environment, and the privacy to spiral as I see fit no longer hold the appeal they did only ten minutes ago.

I'm an author. *A good one.* My career was made from my ability to find the exact right words, yet my dead friend's daughter, this woman whom I've loved as a niece all her life, has robbed me of every last one of them. I have no idea what to do to begin fixing this or if I even should.

All I know for sure is that I want to.

As she strides past me into the hall, preparing to leave, I call after her, "Savvy?" Her shoulders stiffen as she pauses, looking quizzically back at me. I swallow. "Could I ask you a bit of an odd favor?"

"Uh." Her eyebrows pull together. "I guess?"

I nod to the basement door, and suddenly, my pulse is racing. "Could you open that and tell me what you smell?"

Savvy hesitates, nibbling on her bottom lip. I can see she wants to get out of here and probably avoid me for another nine years, but I must have bought myself some good will.

Slowly, she moves back into the kitchen and crosses to the door in question.

Something lodges in my throat as she pulls it open, bracing her hands on the doorframe so she can lean forward, giving the space a little sniff. Her eyelids flutter. "It's nice."

My fists tighten in my pockets, stretching the irritated skin. "Nice?"

She nods, a pretty, pink flush painting her cheeks as she closes the door and turns back to face me, her expression guarded. "Yes. I like it."

Oh.

A dark and unfamiliar feeling is rising inside me, one I'm positive I've never experienced before and wouldn't be able to name if my life depended on it.

I want to say something else, want to draw this out for even another few minutes. Savvy has already resumed her escape, though, obviously just as keen on leaving as I am on keeping her here.

"I'll keep you updated," she promises without looking at me. Her footsteps echo off the high, white walls as she moves out of sight, picking up pace when she hits the entryway, as if she can't get away from me fast enough.

I wince as the door closes with a heavy thud. She's gone.

And she's taken all the warmth in the room with her.

CHAPTER 3
SAVVY

IT'S POURING by the time I make it to Dar's.

There's no point in messing with my makeup, considering I'll be soaked the moment I get out of my car, but I can't resist running my hands through my damp hair a few times, gazing at my reflection in the rearview mirror.

It's always like this before I see him, an undercurrent of restlessness and nervous energy simmering below the surface. I want to be mature about this, cool, but it's no use. My heart is doing that half-flutter, half-squeeze thing.

Lately, it's been happening a lot more often, but my obsession with Darwin Wilder isn't new. The man has been making me weak in the knees for as long as I can remember. Unfortunately, bouncing back and forth between my parents' houses, coupled with Dar's preference for leaving the house as rarely as possible, meant there were sometimes months in between feeling the heady thrill of anticipation building inside me.

Things are different now.

For one thing, I have an actual reason to be here. Thanks to Dar firing his PA (for *"gross incompetence"* and *"being annoy-*

ing"), I scored the best summer job ever. I also don't have to wait around, hoping and praying that Dad would think to ask Dar if he's up for dinner or a game night.

For another, I'm eighteen now.

My stomach somersaults at the thought, and, giving up on my hair, I step out into the freezing rain. It's midsummer, but by the time I make it up

the stone steps to Dar's front door, my teeth are chattering and goosebumps have erupted all over my body.

I press the doorbell, rubbing my arms to get some warmth back into my stiff limbs.

The frosted glass beside the door is dark. I frown, trying the button again. It's hard to tell over the rain, but I'm fairly sure there was no corresponding ring inside.

My knock isn't answered either, but the room Dar likes to write in is clear across the house, and there's no way he'd be able to hear. I've never just gone in before, but it looks like that's what I'll have to do. I'm only here two afternoons a week, and I refuse to miss one of them because of something as inconsequential as torrential rain and a flash flood warning.

The knob turns under my hand, and I poke my head inside. "Dar?" I call, edging into the clean white foyer and stepping out of my sandals. The house is dark apart from the stormy blue light coming in through the windows, and the air is hot and sticky without the air conditioner running.

Outside, thunder rumbles.

"Dar?" I try again, moving into the hall, which leads further into the house, toward the main living area and Darwin's inner sanctum.

As far as I know, Dad and I are the only people he allows back here apart from himself. As happy as I am to be special to him, it also hurts my heart a little when I imagine Dar going days and days with only himself for company. He says he likes it this way, that he prefers his own company, but I'm not sure I've ever believed that the way Dad does.

Does he look forward to me coming? There are days when I think he does, but others when I feel like a nuisance. Still, Darwin Wilder isn't one to protect other people's feelings, and he's never told me to leave.

I push open the kitchen door, and my heart instantly plunges right into my stomach.

My father's best friend, whom I've never in my whole life seen in less than a long-sleeved shirt and jeans, is standing at the kitchen counter wearing shorts. Wearing only shorts.

A haphazard collection of candles cast a flickering, warm light over the room and its only occupant. He doesn't notice me, too intent on wrestling the cork out of a bottle of wine. It's a good thing, too, because shirtless Darwin was not on my bingo card for today, and I am woefully unprepared.

His broad chest is scattered with dark hair that trails down from his belly button to below the band of his cotton shorts. He isn't a model. He doesn't have a six-pack, or a perfectly tapered waist, or biceps that look like he lifts cars in his spare time. It doesn't matter. Every inch of him is masculine and perfect and right in front of me.

I squirm, unable to tear my eyes from him as blood rushes in my ears. It's only been a few seconds, and already my panties are sticky with the evidence of my body's reaction to him. I'm a virgin—a frustrating side effect from being hung up on a man I can't have—but the way I'm feeling right now… *god*. I would let him do anything he wanted to me.

Imagining brusque, uptight Dar coming undone because of the way I make him feel has been my biggest fantasy for longer than I'll ever admit.

I've imagined crawling under his desk while he's writing and hearing an exasperated sigh from above me as I take his cock in my mouth. "Fine," he'd say, his voice harsh with impatience, even as his breathing grows ragged and his hands tighten in my hair.

I've rubbed my clit to thoughts of him coming up to me from behind, his broad, hard body pressing against mine as he orders me to bend over and take what he gives me.

I've come to thoughts of him so many times, I've practically trained myself to get wet for this man.

In front of me, Dar turns to put the corkscrew back in the drawer, and his eyes catch on me hovering in the doorway. He jerks in surprise, cursing. "Savvy! Shit, you scared me. I'm sorry, I didn't expect you to come in this weather or I'd have left a note on the door. No power, as you can see." He gestures to the dark house, smiling wryly.

"Sorry." I edge a little further into the room, doing my best to appear normal. As if anyone could see this man shirtless and not lose some cognitive function. "I'll go—"

"No," Dar says firmly as he selects a wine glass from the nearest cabinet. "You shouldn't have been driving in this at all. Hang out here, the storm should only last another few hours, then I'll send you home. Don't worry, I'll still pay you for today."

I watch helplessly as he crosses to the kitchen table and pulls a discarded gray T-shirt over his head. "Okay," I manage, acutely aware of how ridiculously soaked my panties are, and knowing it has nothing to do with the rain.

God, I need to get a grip. I'm here all the time, and usually I'm marching around like I've been coming here for years— which I have—but one sighting of a partially naked Dar has me too stunned to move.

Oblivious, he looks over at me and smiles easily. "Do you want to play a game?"

To Do: ☆

~~Find a realtor for GG~~

Meeting with accountant

Find an accountant

Exact revenge on Caleb

Clean literally everything

Fix literally everything

Talk to HIM

CHAPTER 4
SAVVY

"THANKS! Don't forget to leave a rating on the app!" I call after the guy climbing out of my backseat. He hasn't said a single word since I picked him up outside a big office building downtown, choosing instead to stare at his phone screen and grunt when I asked if he wanted the AC on.

The door slams shut, and my shoulders sag.

Today has been endless, and it's not even close to over. I spent the morning at the hardware store buying new locks and fresh cleaning supplies for Galactic Guild, then picked up a six-hour shift on the rideshare app that's been my main source of income for the last few months.

I don't love it. Unfortunately, my degree in English (because pre-med, history, and philosophy didn't work out), checkered work history, and inability to be on time even if my life depended on it hasn't yielded many profitable job offers.

When Galactic Guild is up and running, I'll be there full time, but driving will have to do for now. Even if it allows a lot of time for *thinking*, something I've been resolutely avoiding since I left Darwin's house three days ago.

Seeing him again… I was determined not to let it affect me, but it did. It *really* did.

Not just because the man is gorgeous, with his dark hair—that always seems to be perfectly tousled regardless of the humidity level—broad shoulders, and sharp, angular features that are only slightly softened by his dark beard. With all that going for him, nobody could blame me for being attracted to Darwin Wilder, but the truth is a lot more embarrassing than that.

As much as I like to pretend it wasn't the case, once upon a time, I was in love with my father's oldest friend.

It wasn't a crush, or infatuation, or some kind of youthful obsession. I wish it had been, maybe then I would have recovered from it, but no. Facts are facts, and the fact is that by the tender age of eighteen, I was head over heels in love with a man I couldn't have.

I messed up a lot before that day, and I've messed up a lot after, but I'm not sure my heart ever fully recovered from being handed over to a man who had no interest in it. The finer details of the last time I saw Darwin Wilder seem to be permanently ingrained in my memory, faithfully shuffling forward whenever I'm at my lowest. Like now.

My fingers tighten on the steering wheel as I turn my car toward Galactic Guild.

It was a special horror to walk back into that house, the scene of the crime, all but begging for his help. Everything was the same as I remembered it, a time capsule of one of the worst days of my life, and all it took was knocking on the door for the memories to come rushing right back.

Just seeing his face… I wanted to run. I wanted to run so far that I'd never, ever have to look into those cold, dark eyes again, knowing that my being there at all was confirmation of what he said to me nine years ago.

Is there anything worse than knowing that the person who hurt you the most was totally and completely right? It turns out there is, and it's realizing you're still attracted to them.

Haven't I been through enough lately? Is the emotional groin kick necessary?

Thankfully, a distraction arrives in the form of Raven's name on my car's caller ID, and I hit accept before the first ring has even finished.

"Hey, you!" she sings before I can say a word. "Are you done for the day?"

I make a face at the dark road ahead of me. "*Ha.* I wish. Just heading to Galactic Guild now. I'm doing *the bathroom* tonight."

I still haven't ventured in there since my ill-fated attempt to make use of it last week. Just the memory makes me queasy, and this is coming from a girl who

was once convinced to go dumpster diving for dinner (and a side order of salmonella) with her crunchy ex-boyfriend.

While I've entertained the idea of boarding the room up and making my customers pee in the woods, I'm assuming that would negatively affect business.

A pile of crusty poop will not be my downfall. I refuse.

Raven cackles. "It's Savvy Laurence versus Caleb's caca, round two." She drops her voice, adopting the theatrical drawl of a wrestling announcer. "Who will come out on top and claim the bathroom domination belt? Only one way to find out, folks! Stick around for when they go head-to-head in *the stall!*"

"You're the worst."

"Obviously," she agrees cheerfully. "So, have you heard from *him*?"

A sour taste fills my mouth. "You can say his name, and no. I haven't." Nor do I expect to beyond the weekly updates

I promised him. "He's doing me a massive favor. I should be grateful and leave it at that."

That's what I've been telling myself anyway, that it was good of Dar to agree to help at all. I'm positive he's good on money, what with the massive TV show premiering next year and the best-selling books. Selling Galactic Guild at a loss wouldn't cripple him the way it would me, and there is no guarantee spending more would recoup his investment. Still, he'd agreed.

Why?

Was it out of loyalty to Dad or just because of the money? It certainly wasn't out of any kind of fondness for *me*.

I shove the thought away.

It doesn't matter why. Not really. Trying to gain any insight into the inner workings of Darwin Wilder's mind would be a waste of time. He threw me a lifeline, and I'm not proud enough to turn it down.

Raven lets out a long, heavy sigh. "We're busy this weekend. Jonah's boss invited us to his lake house, and then there's that wedding the week after. We'll drive up and help you clean soon, though, and my parents offered to help too. We'll get the place up and running in no time."

I'm glad Raven can't see the tears in my eyes. Her moms, Penny and Julia, are the best people on the planet, and her boyfriend, Jonah, is a close third. I love all of them, they're family to me, but I still have to bite back the urge to turn down their help.

Would I ever hesitate to pitch in for one of them? *Of course not.* So why does the thought of showing weakness, or relying on anyone, make a hot ball of shame open up inside me?

I wipe my eyes with the backs of my hands. "That's so nice of you guys."

"Hey, none of that," Raven says, and I let out a watery laugh. This interfering jerk always knows when I'm crying.

"We've been friends too long."

She snickers. "Yeah, you're right. Time to call it. That one girl at work is always trying to hang out with me. Maybe I'll give her a shot."

"If you do that, I'll leave threatening notes under her windshield wipers until she relinquishes my bestie."

"Super healthy."

"I know, right?"

We fall silent as I pull into my new favorite spot outside the strip mall. The karate place is all lit up with dozens of kids in white uniforms and colored belts running around inside, but next door, Galactic Guild is conspicuously dark and still.

Not for long. I've spent the last few nights cleaning the lobby and finalizing the list of what needs to be done before we reopen. The list is intimidating, but doable.

"I should let you go. Just got here," I tell Raven, watching the kids romp around next door, laughing and wild, as wistfulness and regret twist painfully inside me.

Was I ever that carefree?

If I was, I don't remember. Most of my earliest memories are of trying to hide my shitty grades from my parents or saying something awkward in the middle of science class and shriveling up when the pretty blonde girls next to me exchanged *that look*. I was weird, and a little dorky, and my dad sent me to school in vintage sci-fi T-shirts instead of Gap, but that wasn't the reason I didn't have many friends.

I *wish* I could blame my unpopularity on something external and out of my control, but people didn't like me because of *me*. Because I blurted out the wrong things at the wrong time and could never quite read the room. If it weren't for Raven, I wouldn't have had a single friend, and I'll never forget that she's stuck by my side since pre-school, even when I'm positive she could have found cooler friends.

Now, she has a great job in the closest city, a cute apartment, a cat named Arnold, and a boyfriend who is both hot *and* respectful. My best friend has her shit together, but she still doesn't judge me for having to cut open the end of my toothpaste tubes to scrape the last remnants.

I definitely don't deserve her.

"I'll see you next Saturday, okay?" she says, her voice determinately cheerful, undoubtedly trying to offset my plummeting mood.

Though she can't see me, I nod. "Okay. Thanks, Rave. Love you." "Love you back."

I end the call, staring into the dark windows of my business. God, it's so weird to call it that, but it is. *Mine*, for better or worse.

A small, bitter corner of my brain wonders if that's why Dar agreed to pay for this. Maybe he wants final confirmation of what a fuckup I am. It's a stupid thought, even my bitter ass knows that, but it's enough to spark a defiant sort of determination inside me.

Not waiting around for it to fade, I shove open the car door and step out into the warm summer air.

A few of the karate parents are waiting in their cars, and I feel their eyes on me as I haul two armfuls of cleaning supplies up to the dark door. I shoot them a sheepish smile over my shoulder as I fumble with my key, as though that will make me look any less like I'm cleaning up after a murder.

According to the marketing podcast I've been listening to, these people are my target customers. They want to shove their kids through the door with enough money for cheap pizza and some games so they can steal a few minutes of well-deserved silence.

I'm not a parent, but I don't think I'd send my child to a sketchy, possible crime scene run by a pink-haired lunatic.

It's a good thing I thought to tape sheets of paper over the big front windows, because nothing about how this place looks right now is going to dispel that impression. I'm still not used to being here alone, with all the arcade games silent and the ghostly shapes of aliens and starships leering at me through the darkness.

It's just so *still*. Even my footsteps, muffled on the faded purple carpet, seem unnaturally loud, and every *thud* of a car door closing outside makes my heart jump into my throat.

Apparently, the bill for the alarm company hasn't been paid in over a year, so the deadbolt better work until money is coming in and I can

reconnect the service. I refuse to spend Darwin's money on anything that isn't essential, even if that means walking around with the tiny hairs on the back of my neck standing on end.

I shake myself as I set the cleaning supplies on the counter of the snack bar, then move past it to flick on the fluorescent overhead lights. This action might make it slightly less creepy, but improving visibility does not do this place any favors or discourage the inevitable crime-scene rumors.

It's nothing I can't handle. Or, at least, that's the lie I keep telling myself whenever the panic sets in.

The only room I'm determined not to enter alone is the actual laser tag arena. It lies behind a set of double doors and a briefing room—where players learn the rules of the game, get assigned to teams, and are outfitted with their weaponry.

It's huge in there, full of places to hide, bridges, and barrels of fake radioactive waste. Raven and I snuck a quick peek, and even with the overhead lights on, and no flashing lasers, fake smoke, or pulsing music, it's eerie.

I'm just at the point of pouring cleaner into a mop bucket when the soft brush of the door opening over the entryway mat makes my heart leap into my throat. Turning wildly, I only narrowly avoid falling on my ass beside the gallon of cleaner, which is now spilling everywhere.

I have bigger problems, though, because there's a tall,

broad-shouldered man standing in the doorway, his hands shoved deep in his pockets as he frowns at me.

"Darwin," I hiss, pressing a hand over my racing heart. *"Holy fuck."*

"Sorry." A deep frown pulls at the corners of his lips as he watches me scoop up the bottle.

My pulse is still thudding unevenly as I get to my feet. "You're, um, here?" Instantly, heat rushes to my face. What is it about this man that makes me say and do such stupid things?

Darwin doesn't seem to notice, though. He's too busy examining the mural to my right, a galactic battle depicted in bright neon colors. After an age, he turns his gaze back to me, and something low in my stomach gives a little flip.

I ignore it.

"I hope you don't mind," he says, and outside his natural habitat, his voice has lost some of its authority.

Dad once told me that Darwin has "issues". He hadn't said it meanly, but it was clear enough what he meant. In all the years we knew Darwin, I can only remember seeing him outside the house a handful of times, and he'd been visibly uncomfortable for all of them. Then there were the periods when he didn't want us to visit at all, or when the house smelled so strongly of disinfectant that it made my head spin and my skin itch.

Which makes it even more confusing that he's here now.

We're only a few miles down the road, but this place is a universe away from his obsessively clean, contemporary house full of sharp angles and glossy white paint.

I blink, trying to come up with some reason he'd come here. "Did you need to see the receipts?"

"Receipts?"

"For what I spent on your card," I clarify, turning to my makeshift desk on the snack bar's counter. Little slips of paper generally get shoved in the center console of my car and used for gum disposal, but I've been careful to account for every penny I've spent so far.

When I find the folder and hold it out, though, Dar just frowns. "That's not why I'm here."

He doesn't elaborate, and as the silence stretches on, I feel a prickle of annoyance. Did he just come to see the train wreck for himself? "I have a lot of work to do," I say waspishly, planting my hands on my hips.

"Yes." His throat bobs. "I thought you might like some help."

For a moment, all I can do is blink at him, trying to think of other possible meanings for that particular combination of words.

"Help?" I choke belatedly, "With… this?" I gesture around at the dusty lobby, not bothering to disguise the disbelief in my voice.

Darwin nods jerkily, even as a nerve in his forehead twitches, repulsion evident in every tense inch of his body. He's strung tight, a bow ready to snap. "Correct."

I cross my arms, struggling to comprehend why he would want to be involved with any of this. "You don't like germs. Or people. Or loud noises." *Or me.*

Dar's head bobs. "Also correct."

"So, why—"

He scowls. "As you said, you don't have experience with this sort of thing. I think it would be better if I took the lead."

My mouth pops open.

Is he joking right now? Of course he isn't. Darwin Wilder doesn't joke. He's as straightlaced as they come, and the stone-cold serious expression on his face confirms it.

Maybe these supplies will clean up a murder after all.

"Okay. Fine." Sucking in a deep, steadying breath, I continue, "You have every right to be here. It's your business too." It's pretty impressive how calm I sound right now, despite how I'm resisting the impulse to hurl something at his stupid face.

His stupid face that I stupidly still find handsome. Goddammit. *Why is everyone here so stupid?*

I try again. "But… Darwin. You have to know, it's *disgusting* in here. The manager Dad hired when he got sick didn't give half a crap. Trust me, you don't want to do this. *I* don't want to do this. If you don't believe me, stick around to watch me clean the bathroom."

Dar's jaw tightens, and there's a steely, defiant look on his face now. "I'll clean the bathroom. It's not a problem."

He's apparently trying to prove something right now, either to himself or to me.

Instead of easing himself into facing his phobias like every therapist on the planet would probably recommend, he's going straight for the Satan's butthole of bathrooms.

On the other hand, maybe I can make this work for me. He's determined to do it. I did my moral duty in telling him it was a bad idea, but he doesn't trust my judgment.

If the giant prick wants to "take the lead" on this, he can be my guest.

I hitch a broad, fake smile on my face and march over to where he's standing to shove a bottle of bathroom cleaner and a roll of paper towels into his gloved hands. "Do you know what? Fine. Go for it."

He blinks in surprise, evidently expecting me to put up more of a fight. "Now?"

"Yup." I point unnecessarily toward the back hall. "Have fun. I'm not sure I'm experienced enough to handle it yet, but I'm betting you can, Mister Big-Time Author. Didn't they call you a genius in that *Times* profile? *Wow!* Color me impressed. Don't let someone like *me* hold you back."

Darwin just stares at me, and I can practically hear the wheels in his mind turning.

"Chop, chop!" I chirp, and the smile I'm wearing isn't fake anymore.

He stares at me for a moment before slowly turning in the direction I indicated.

My grin doesn't slip an inch as he walks out of sight, clutching the supplies I pushed on him. Ordinarily, I'm very respectful of people's eccentricities—I have enough of my own to be sympathetic—but I can be a ruthless asshole when the occasion calls for it, and Darwin Wilder deserves it.

Seriously, why does he have to be so *mean*? What happened between us was nine years ago, and before that —*bang!*

Down the hall, I hear the unmistakable sound of a bathroom door being thrown back open. Seconds later, Darwin stumbles back into view, his face chalk white and lips pressed together like he's trying not to vomit all over the carpet.

Oops.

"Yeah." I sigh in a clearly fake show of sympathy. "It's a shit show. No pun intended."

Darwin looks like he's going to puke, though, and reluctantly, I feel a twinge of regret. Also, concern for the carpet.

Goddammit, I really need to work on my ruthless asshole side.

I groan. "Come on." Marching forward, I loop my hand through his elbow, tugging the giant of a man back through the lobby and outside into the fresh air. "Sit down." I push down on his shoulders so he's forced to fold his long limbs into a seated position on the curb.

He curses under his breath in between panting. "That was appalling." "*Appalling*," I echo, and sit beside him, the asphalt crunching under my sneakers. "Always the writer, Mr. Wilder."

It's a perfect, warm summer's night, the kind that makes you think of soft-serve ice cream and fireflies. Kids are laughing in the karate place, and I'm sitting side by side with a man whom I hoped never to see again.

"I'm sorry," he says, and there's a low strain in his voice, as though every word is costing him.

I turn so fast that my neck twinges. "For what?"

Darwin's lips flatten into a grave line, but he keeps his eyes on the asphalt beneath our feet. "For what I said. About taking the lead. I… I didn't come here to say that. I'm sorry."

Huh.

He's apologizing to me, so why do I suddenly feel vulnerable? I swallow. "So why did you? Come here, I mean."

"To say the opposite." He smiles wryly, turning his gaze to a car backing out of the parking spot across from us. "It doesn't seem fair that you shoulder the burden of Stone's choices alone. Especially when I'm far more to blame for this than you are."

I turn my gaze back to the parking lot. "You're already helping more than you need to."

"No. I'm not. I—" His voice falters, as though he's struggling to find the right words. Cool, controlled Darwin, who always seems to know what to do, is as rattled by all this as I am. "I thought we could be partners."

Silence stretches between us, and I drag my sneaker over a pebble, my heart in my throat. A tiny, pathetic part of me is so relieved at what he's offering. Wasn't it only a few days ago that I wished for someone to save me from this mess?

But, how could he? There isn't a single job in the building that wouldn't make his skin crawl. By the look of his hands, his compulsions are *not* under control.

I swallow. "You saw how bad it is, Dar. I don't want you to be uncomfortable."

It's pretty high talk from someone who just sent him into the bathroom of doom, but I mean it. The only thing worse than Darwin being here as a superior, controlling jerk is

Darwin being here to actually help me and hating every second of it.

Besides, there's no way he wants to be around me. Nine years of radio silence seem like pretty convincing evidence of that. He doesn't need the money, either, so why would he put himself through this?

I hazard another peek at his profile, expecting to see him staring off into the night, but my heart flips when I meet his eyes instead. Neither of us turn away.

We're so close, I can see that there are a few strands of gray woven through the temples of his dark hair and tiny lines branching out from the corners of his eyes. He looks older than I remember, but it suits him. He's handsome. *Too handsome.*

I wonder what he sees when he looks at me. A mess, probably.

"I've been comfortable for a long time, Savvy, and it hasn't made me happy," Darwin admits quietly. "I think it's time to try something else." Slowly, like he's trying to work himself up to it, he holds out a gloved hand in the small distance between us. "What do you say? Partners?"

This feels like a trap. Every instinct I have is screaming: *No! Turn back! Danger!*

I don't listen. I never do.

Reaching across the small space between us, I take his hand.

I *hate* that it makes my pulse race and warmth spread through my veins.

I *hate* that I know very well that this may turn out terribly, but I'm doing it anyway.

I *hate* that when I open my mouth and say the words that will bind me to Darwin Wilder for the foreseeable future, the world seems to tilt on its axis, and the teeniest, tiniest bit of hope flickers to life inside me.

"Okay," I agree. "Partners."

CHAPTER 5
DARWIN

"CAN I HELP YOU?"

The keys to Galactic Guild dangle precariously from one finger as I approach the door, arms laden with an assortment of industrial-grade cleaning supplies, purchased last week as weaponry in my war against The Smell.

It's the early hours of afternoon, hours before school lets out, and the strip mall is a ghost town. Savvy isn't here yet, and my car is alone in the parking lot. I was counting on not running into anyone, and I certainly wasn't expecting to encounter a group of strange teenagers.

They're clustered beside the front door, watching me approach with expressions ranging from awe to disbelief.

The boldest among them, a girl with wild black hair and about a dozen piercings on each ear, steps forward. "Shit, you're Darwin Wilder, aren't you?" she gasps, eyes practically bugging out of her head.

I suppress a wince. Fame, at least in certain circles, was an unintended and unwelcome byproduct of my books' rise in popularity. My publisher, who seemed to believe my face would help sales, insisted on splashing my headshot across every available platform. Thankfully, a small city in upstate New York has a sparse population of science-fiction fans, and I've been able to fly under the radar for years.

My standing practice of leaving the house as seldom as possible is also helpful.

I should have expected that luxury to end. Of course, whatever sci-fi fans this town does have would gravitate to a laser tag arena named *Galactic Guild*. Not only that, but I know for a fact that Stone hosted gaming tournaments, DnD campaigns, and all sorts of events that would almost certainly attract people who read my books.

"Yes, I am." I attempt a polite smile that must look more like a grimace, setting down the bottles of disinfectant so I can fumble with the keys Savvy (with obvious reluctance) entrusted to me last night. The black latex gloves I'm wearing make the job difficult, but the kids are too busy exchanging wide-eyed looks to notice.

"Did you buy this place?" asks their leader, her voice going high with excitement. "Did you know Stone?"

"I did, and yes. He was an old friend." The key turns in the lock, and I stoop to grab the bottles before shouldering open the door. I expect that to be the end of the conversation, but it isn't. All five teens follow me inside.

"We're not open," I point out unnecessarily. There are boxes of supplies and tools all over the place, and the lobby is lit only by the glow of the grimy Pepsi coolers.

When I flip the lights, it gets worse.

After I left last night, Savvy began ripping up the stained carpet around the snack bar. By the looks of it, she got bored halfway through and switched to changing fluorescent light bulbs, which also isn't finished.

I force myself to take a long, steady breath, focusing on the feeling of the air filling my lungs and leaving them instead of the hot panic crawling up my spine.

"So, did Harcrow really die in *The Reckoning of Kaul*?" asks another girl eagerly, and I turn to face them. As tempting as it is to tell the group to leave, a distraction wouldn't be unwelcome.

I exhale heavily and nod. "The series is over. So yes." There are some nods and approving murmurs to this.

Another chips in, "What about Delfi? Is she going to be happy being an empress after working as a rebel for so long?"

I blink. "I think it's more—" "But when Nemo pulled Kaul—"

"No dummy, Jorin pushed Kaul!"

"Nemo's last name *is* Jorin, idiot! Did you even read the books?" The bickering intensifies, and so does the throbbing in my temples.

"What are you all doing here?" I finally demand, raising my voice to be heard above the debate.

Five sets of eyes look to me. "Stone *always* let us play DnD in the back room," says the girl with the ear piercings, and her bottom lip trembles. "We haven't been able to since this place closed. Luke and King's parents are total dickwads who think we're worshiping the devil or something, and my mom's apartment is super small, and—"

"I get it." I hold up a hand to stop her.

It doesn't surprise me in the least that Stone gave these kids a safe place to play. Hell, a few decades ago, he and I were the ones desperately trying to hold a campaign together when all our parents thought we were better off playing football.

Grief and guilt twist bitterly inside me, a physical pain I'm still not used to.

For weeks, I've been prowling around the house, my compulsions resurfacing in the wake of Stone's death and the completion of my series, canceling one therapy appointment after another. Gone was my life's work, and the only true friend I've ever had. Is it any wonder I was ready to attack the walls?

Now, if only I could so easily rationalize Savvy's effect on me.

I'd thought it was a fluke, a reaction brought on by isolation and whatever mental break I was suffering from when she showed up on my doorstep.

Coming here last night… For the first time in my meticulously ordered life, I didn't have a plan. Not really. Mostly, I wanted to prove to myself that I *could* leave the house if I really wanted to. I also wanted confirmation that it *wasn't* attraction I felt toward Savvy. Because it couldn't be.

I've spent days convincing myself of all that, but it only took walking through the door of Galactic Guild to eviscerate my last ties to normalcy. My reaction to her hadn't lessened; it intensified.

So much so that, within the space of a few minutes, I'd insulted her, almost vomited on her shoes, offered to be her business partner, and all but admitted I've been depressed.

I've never spoken to another person like that. *Ever.* As a child, my parents joked I had more secrets than the Pentagon. Even Stone never pushed me to open up any more than I did to him. God knows romantic relationships were off the table, so I've stayed closed off and never questioned it. My objection to most of the human population isn't only because of my disorder, but it hasn't helped matters.

So, after forty-five years of this, what is it about Savvy Laurence that is making me say and do things I've never even considered before?

Christ, I don't remember the last time I touched another person, even with gloves on. Yet the weight of Savvy's hand in mine didn't make my stomach roll or sweat gather on the back of my neck. I didn't feel the burning urge to scrub my skin until it's red or pour antiseptic over the places she touched.

The ugly, confusing truth is that *I liked it,* and I have no idea what I'm supposed to do with that. I have more than a fair amount of experience in distracting myself from mental spirals, but abandoning thoughts of Savvy isn't happening.

I clear my throat, gazing around at the assembled teenagers. "Listen, I'll talk to my business partner, but I'm sure she won't have a problem with it once we reopen."

"When's that?" asks the smallest of the group, a boy whose neck seems to be fifty percent Adam's apple. They're all grinning, though, and exchanging wide-eyed, significant looks.

"No idea." I move past them and reopen the door. "Soon. Hopefully. There's a lot that needs to be done."

The checklist Savvy has going is intimidating, to say the least.

They've hardly begun filing back outside when the smallest boy leaps to the side. A second later, Savvy appears, a massive box wedged under her chin and a pencil sticking out of her messy bun.

Pausing in the doorway, she frowns over her box at the group of teenagers. "Is one of you Caleb?"

There are a few confused mutters, and one of them pipes up, "Uh, no?"

Savvy nods, satisfied. "Okay. Good." She strides past me, and a beat too late, I realize I ought to have taken the box from her.

I'm positive I feel eyes following me as I trail after her to the snack bar area, but when I tear my eyes away from her to check, the teens have gone. The door closes, and suddenly Savvy and I are alone.

"What was all that about?" she asks over her shoulder, already busy ripping packing tape from cardboard.

Is she trying to avoid meeting my eye?

I clear my throat, hating that it bothers me. "Apparently, your father let them play DnD in the birthday party room when nobody was using it. I think they were checking to see if we'd let it continue."

"Oh yeah, he told me about them. Of course they can play. Maybe we should look into adding some formal tabletop rooms." Her voice is determinately casual, and—yeah—that can work. I can do casual. No problem.

I can *not* notice the way her T-shirt clings to the curve of her waist, or how those stretchy shorts she's wearing do nothing to hide the shape of her ass. None of that is relevant or welcome. An adolescent crush doesn't translate to reciprocated attraction nine years later, especially not for a man twice her age who's been too busy battling his own malfunctioning brain and obsessing over fictional characters to learn how to connect with actual human beings.

A man who hurt her.

That day has haunted me for years, but the longer we went without seeing each other... I thought she'd be embarrassed about the whole thing, but would ultimately forget it. I thought that reaching out and apologizing would soothe my conscience, but would do nothing for hers.

I never imagined it would be nine years before I saw her again, or that those words I spat in anger and shock might have wounded her so deeply that she still struggles to meet my eye.

Does she know those things weren't really about her? She doesn't believe them, does she? Or think that I do?

I rock back onto my heels, struggling to piece together the best course of action while the shock of my *painfully* real attraction is still so fresh.

"What are you doing?" I ask, purely to distract us both from the uncomfortable silence. "Do you need help?"

"Uh, I don't think so." Savvy tosses what appears to be the instruction manual onto the pile of packaging trash on the floor. "It's just the new vacuum cleaner. I looked into fixing the one that's here now, but it looks like a small creature made a home in it, and I don't think there's any coming back from that."

A nerve in my forehead twitches. We're standing amidst at least half a dozen partially completed projects, but as infuriating as I find it that she won't finish one of them first, I keep my mouth shut. Savvy has her way of doing things, and I have mine. I sure as hell am in no position to give orders or ruffle her feathers so early on.

Still, I'm uncomfortable. For such a large room, the stillness makes the air feel oppressive and heavy. I've been here for less than five minutes, and already I'm itching to step back outside, or better yet, get in my car and return to my safe, familiar house with its expensive air-filtration system.

To distract myself, I flip on the lights in the massive arcade room and they flicker to life, illuminating the space in black light. Closest to me, a row of claw machines stand dark and silent, their ghostly contents barely distinguishable.

Stone is everywhere.

I see my late friend grinning over his shoulder at me as he empties quarters from the pinball machine into a bucket.

His booming laugh echoes over the voices of excited children, shaking his head as he reaches over the prize counter to hand a little girl a stuffed dolphin that's twice her size.

He's sitting at the snack bar, where his daughter stands now, gray faced and telling me his wife left him.

This place was Stone's home, a place of magic in his eyes, and that's why it made it so long, even if my friend was the world's shittiest businessman.

We didn't talk about Galactic Guild in his last days. Though now, in retrospect, I know he must have felt horrible guilt for the financial situation he left Savvy in. I'd offered to come to the hospital, to brave the city and hospital super germs to visit him, but he'd assured me Savvy was there and I… I hadn't wanted to distract from her last days with her father.

As far as I'm aware, Stone never knew what transpired between us nine years ago, and I didn't think his death bed was a good place for that story to come to light. I don't regret it. Especially now, when I've seen firsthand what nearly a decade of silence can do to buried pain and regret. And the very non-platonic feelings my surrogate niece now inspires in me.

Blinking away memories of Stone, I stare around at the still room. There are at least six games with "out of order" signs taped to them, and a bucket of dirty water stationed below what is clearly a roof leak. Everywhere I look there are problems, and, for the first time since I so rashly offered Savvy my help, I'm second-guessing if I can do it.

This place is overwhelming, and who the hell am I to try and fix anything? For fuck's sake, only a few days ago, I was prepared to take a sledgehammer to my basement drywall to get rid of The Smell. Galactic Guild has far more and worse problems.

Then there's the fact that the woman in charge of solving them is a human tornado, likely intent on my destruction.

Stupid. So unbelievably, undeniably stupid. What the hell was I thinking? Panic is tightening in my throat, obstructing my breathing, and so is the urgency to go home and scrub every inch of my body. I *need* to get out of here.

"Are you freaking out?"

I spin around. Savvy is standing just behind me, her arms crossed and a wry smile playing on her lips. Even her beauty isn't enough to distract me.

"We need to hire professionals, Savvy," I tell her, shaking my head. "This is too much. It doesn't matter how much it costs—I don't care—but we can't..." I gesture around. It doesn't matter where I point, it will be toward something that needs fixing.

Far from looking relieved, or even affronted, Savvy just stares up at me. My mostly unused heart flips when a slight, understanding smile curves her lips. In the black lights from the arcade, her hair looks like it's glowing, and I—What was it that sent me spiraling? It seemed so important a moment ago, but now I've lost the thread.

"It's good for the plot, Dar," she says simply, and I hear the startled laugh coming from my mouth as though it's someone else's.

I'm reeling. Of all the things she could have said… My heart beats faster.

Years ago, when a fifteen-year-old Savvy interviewed me for an English project, I'd explained my writing process. I'd joked that when things would inevitably go awry, it's good for the plot, because I'm at my best when there's a problem to solve.

I can't believe she remembers that.

Having my own words used against me is something of an occupational hazard, but not like this. Never like this.

"Come on." Savvy nods back to the snack bar. "There's a million parts to that thing. It's terrible. I could use your help."

I find myself hoping she'll loop her hand through my arm like last night, but she doesn't.

Mutely, I follow her, preoccupied by that moment.

Until a few days ago, I was comfortable in the way my mind worked. It was familiar, triggered by the same things and calmed by others, but now everything is off. I'm obsessing over things I've never even considered before, feeling things I thought I couldn't.

And, at the center of it all, is Savvy.

Change doesn't come easily to me, and I've avoided it as much as possible for my entire adult life. This woman has been back in my life for less than a week, and everything is different. She's a tornado. I should be hunkering down in my basement, but instead I'm driving right into it yelling, *Take me!*

I stoop to rescue the owner's manual from a pile of discarded packaging on the floor.

Savvy's already unpacked all the parts and attachments,

and I move to her side, scanning through the assembly directions. "It's not so bad," I tell her, reaching for the first part I need and kneeling to attach it as directed.

As I look up in search of another, my eyes catch on a tiny flash of black ink under the arm of her cut T-shirt.

She has a tattoo? Of what?

As my eyes fall back to the vacuum, Savvy huffs, "It looks like the inside of The Drake."

It takes a moment for her words to sink in, but when they do, my hands still. I look up at her. "You read my books?"

She crosses her arms, a dull flush painting her cheeks, and her eyes fall to a clipboard on the counter. When she finally replies, her voice is too casual to be entirely convincing. "Yeah, of course I did. You knew that. For my fifteenth birthday, I bullied you into giving me an advanced copy of book four, remember?"

Yes, but I've published three books in the years since —*since*. The book she just referenced came out seven years ago, and, judging by that blush, my little tornado knows it. I would have expected that she wouldn't have wanted to read my words with how we left things.

She did, though. *She read them*, and that fact alone makes me happier than any high-profile review or landing on a bestseller list.

"What did you think?" I'm pushing my luck and, based on the waspish look I get in response, Savvy agrees.

"I think I'm going to go crack the bathroom door and pour a bucket of bleach inside to see what happens."

As I turn back to the vacuum, I'm smiling. "Sounds like a plan."

To Do: ☆

~~Find a realtor for GG~~

~~Meeting with accountant~~

~~Find an accountant~~

Exact revenge on Caleb

Clean literally everything

Fix literally everything

~~Talk to HIM~~

~~New Vacuum~~

Rip up stained carpet in lobby+snackbar

Replace those long lightbulbs in the ceiling

Find out which games in arcade don't work

Fix roof leak

Reconnect security system (at some point)

CHAPTER 6
SAVVY

T'S BEEN a week since Darwin showed up at Galactic Guild.

When he said he'd help, I assumed it would be a *show up to pitch in every now and again* kind of thing. It was pretty obvious he was in an awful place when I turned up at his house, and even if I'm determined not to feel bad for him (or feel anything at all for Darwin Wilder), something inside me pinches whenever I remember his poor hands.

As far as I know, Dad was the only non-professional connection he had in his life. They were friends for longer than I've been alive. Stress and grief were bound to affect his mental health, and the fact he was so isolated… Well. He was obviously here to get himself in order, a little exposure therapy to the outside world, while biding his time before the next great idea sent him back into his writing hole.

I could deal with that.

What I *can't* deal with is keeping my shit together for hours on end every day.

Look, it's not like I'm a complete basket case. I have some sense of self-awareness and control. But, if you're around *anyone* long enough, you're going to see them make a mistake. They'll do something monumentally stupid, or klutzy, or forgetful. It's normal to have those moments, like, *Oops! I forgot my doctor's appointment!* or, *Darn, I knocked over my glass of wine.*

Unfortunately, in my case, that time is bound to come sooner rather than later. Also, given twenty-seven years of experience in living with myself, I know those mistakes won't be so cute. We're looking at something a lot closer to, *Whoops! Stabbed myself in the foot!* or, *Gosh darn it, I mixed cleaning supplies and created a chemical weapon! Don't you hate it when that happens?*

Normally, I don't care. Really. I've made my peace with being an idiot. Unfortunately, I'm a *proud* idiot. A proud idiot who is now spending hours alone with the one person whom I don't want privy to that deeply unfortunate quality, because Darwin *keeps showing up.*

It's not a phase. It's not even exposure therapy, because he stopped wearing his gloves days ago. His hands look better, still painful even to look at, but the redness has gone down and I've only seen him wash them a few times since he started coming here. He's been focusing on repairing the broken machines in the arcade, which is fine by me, because I certainly don't have the patience for it.

I really didn't expect it to last, but night after night, we work side by side, mostly in silence. There are times he makes an offhand comment, or I do, and it sparks a bit of perfectly civil conversation.

And, sometimes, that perfectly civil conversation turns into us actually talking.

There's so much about Darwin that I'd forgotten, little habits or the way he can make me laugh with his dry, humorless comments. While no one could accuse Darwin Wilder of being charming, I can hardly blame my younger self for falling for him, even if there was—*is*—a million reasons not to. Like it or not, we understand each other, and it's been an effort not to fall back into the rhythm of the easy, familiar friendship we once had.

None of that means I can allow myself to forget the reason for our nine-year estrangement. I want this man to see me as an adult, a peer, and not the same impulsive girl he sent running from his home that rainy night nine years ago.

Regrettably for me, *impulsive* may as well be my middle name. I've tried to change, tried to curb my behavior. All goes well until I get this *great idea*, which turns out to be not such a great idea, and my life is fucked up once again.

It's why I can't keep a relationship for longer than six months.

It's why I signed up for my current job on an app that takes anyone with a valid driver's license.

It's why I'm currently scrambling to hide a giant game-show wheel before Darwin gets to Galactic Guild.

"Oh god." I stare up at the thing—which is at least two feet taller than I am—my throat tight with panic.

What was I thinking?

Sure, it was only fifty dollars on Craigslist and seemed like a good deal. But this is exactly the kind of nonsense I'm trying to avoid. There are a million things to do around here, and responsible, logical adults focus on those first.

They do not drive forty-five minutes to buy a game-show wheel from some guy named Jerry, strap it to the roof of their sedan, drive back going twenty miles below the speed limit, and enlist a group of karate students to help them get it inside.

I had so many opportunities to abort this mission. So many chances to sit back, look at what I was doing, and consider *maybe* it wasn't the best use of my time.

Thankfully, the wheel is on wheels.

Looking around wildly, my eyes catch on the large double doors to the arena, and my heart leaps. I don't think Darwin has ventured in there at all. Perfect.

Hey, maybe I can say I found it and blame it on Stone. That's not horrible, is it? Blaming your poor decisions on your dead dad so his best friend, whom you once threw yourself at and he brutally rejected you, doesn't find out he was right about what a mess you are.

Right now, I don't give a flying fart about the moral integrity of this plan. I just need to make sure Darwin never finds out I spent the better part of my morning finding, buying, and transporting a seven-foot-tall game-show wheel.

Gripping the side, I lean into it and push, shoving the thing over the mostly torn-up carpet in the direction of the only possible hiding spot. The wheel sways, and I wrap my arms around it the best I can to steady it.

Trying again, I proceed slower, craning my neck around the side to foresee any potential hazards in my way. It's working too. I'm rocking this. There's ten feet to go, then five, then two, but when I dart around the front to ease it through the doorway, my mouth falls open in horror, because the stupid wheel is about six inches taller than the doorframe.

No. No. No.

This isn't really happening right now, is it? Six inches will make the difference between me maintaining some shred of dignity or not? I'm so furious, I'm not even going to make a penis joke to myself. Though, of course, thinking about making a penis joke is just as bad as making one, so—*no.* Not now.

I bite my lip, staring up at the wheel as thoughts ping-pong around in my skull, searching for solutions to the problem at hand. Maybe if I could just tilt it onto the back wheels and push it through?

It's the only option. I have to.

My heart is lodged in my throat as I reach up to grab the top and begin easing it back toward myself. It's heavy, but not so heavy that I can't hold it up. I've got this. Everything is fine. If I could just—*oh, fuck.*

Somehow in the formation of this plan, I neglected to consider one very important fact: that wheels spin.

It happens so fast that I don't have time to scramble out of the way. One second, I'm trying to ease the tilted wheel through the doors, and the next, the wheels have slipped out from under it, and I'm falling. My back hits the floor so hard it pushes the air from my lungs. Or, maybe it wasn't so much the fall as it was the massive, wooden wheel landing on top of me.

Disoriented and wheezing, I blink up at the ceiling, struggling to catch up with this turn of events. Only my head and shoulders are poking out from beneath the thing, but before I can even think of wiggling out, there's a sharp cry from the direction of the front door.

"Savvy!"

My head thuds back onto the carpet, a resigned sort of mortification settling over me as Darwin's feet and calves come into view. Then, the weight is gone from my chest as my tall, well-built business partner lifts the wheel into an upright position with no struggle whatsoever.

"Are you okay?" he demands, dropping to his knees beside me. Darwin looks, well, frantic. His hands move to my arms, then my head, checking for injuries.

He doesn't even seem to realize, or care, that his bare skin is touching mine.

I lurch away, scrambling to my feet. "Totally fine," I squeak, backing away. "It just happened a second before you came in."

This is humiliating enough without him thinking I laid there for hours, trapped like a turtle on its back.

Darwin gets to his feet, still looking unconvinced. "I think we should get you to the emergency room, just to be sure."

My mouth pops open in horror. "Oh my god, no! Dar, seriously, look." I wave my limbs around theatrically and hop up and down a bit. "I'm fine. Nothing hurts."

Except the back of my head, but I'm not telling him that.

Worried, dark eyes scan my body, searching for signs of distress, and— because there is something deeply wrong with me—my skin tingles under the weight of his gaze. Dar's throat bobs when he finally finishes assuring himself that I'm not dying. "Are you sure?"

I flash him a reassuring smile. "Totally."

"You'll tell me? If anything starts to hurt?"

No way. "Of course."

Silence falls between us, and, as if he's just noticing it for the first time, Darwin's eyes turn to the massive wheel beside me. He blinks, staring at it. "Is that—"

"A game-show wheel?" I suggest, blood rushing to my face. "Yeah." More silence.

"Ah." Darwin rubs his beard, likely trying to find a way to diplomatically call me a basket case. "What are we going to do with it?"

My face must be tomato red right now with how hot it is. "It was a bad idea. I'm going to list it online and see if I can find a buyer."

To my surprise, he frowns. "You must have had a plan when you bought it. Tell me." It's not an order, but there's something in his voice… He really wants to know.

I swallow, reaching over to scratch my nail over the wooden edge distractedly. "So, have you ever heard of speed dating?" The completely blank expression in response to this question confirms I was right not to assume. "Well, it's this event that's usually hosted at a restaurant or bar or something. Single people sign up, and you take turns talking to everyone for a few minutes. If you click with someone, great, and if not, you didn't have to go on a dozen bad dates to find out."

"People *pay* to go to events like this?" he presses, looking disbelieving.

Now, I'm blushing for a whole other reason. "*Yes*. People

want to be loved, to be in relationships. There's nothing wrong with that."

Darwin seems to struggle to accept that statement. "Okay. So, how did we get from speed dating to the giant wheel?"

Despite myself, a hysterical little giggle escapes from between my lips. "Well, I thought we could do that here. Host events a few nights a month. Adults only, obviously. Except they wouldn't be sitting awkwardly across from a stranger, they'd be engaging in an epic battle for intergalactic domination, aided by a teammate who *happens* to be single and wants a relationship just like they do. It would take all night to play with everyone, though. So, I thought it would be fun to put the names of the first half of participants on the wheel and have the second half spin to find out who they're playing with. It's flashy, you know? People would post about it on social media, so that's free advertising for us."

I force myself not to squirm or look away from him. It *is* a pretty good idea, maybe a little hastily thought out, but still. It's not like I bought a seven-foot-tall wheel for no reason. Dar is just staring at me, though, and the longer he does, the more defensive I become. The next thing out of his mouth is going to be disapproving or patronizing. I just know it is.

"That's an amazing idea, Savvy." My pulse thuds in my ears. "*What?*"

"It's great." Darwin crosses his arms and moves so he can see the front of the wheel. "How much would we charge for something like that?"

"Oh." I sway, taken off guard by his approval and totally unwilling to admit it makes me happy. "I was thinking forty dollars a person to cover two games, and maybe some snacks after? We can't serve alcohol without a liquor license, but people could bring their own. We'd keep the arcade open so they can play games after too. Like a mini impromptu date." I shrug, watching as Darwin pulls the wheel, his eyes following the blur of spinning colors.

He looks over at me, his handsome face splitting into a genuine smile. "It's great, Savvy. The perfect way to get people in the door on nights when we ordinarily wouldn't see much business. I can't believe you came up with that and found the wheel and everything. How did you get it here?"

I don't want to smile, really I don't, but my mouth seems to do it against my will. "On the roof of my car."

Darwin snorts, shaking his head like he can picture the absurdity and isn't put off at all. "Call me next time. Okay? At the very least, I can be back-up muscle." The sleeves of his T-shirt, which are stretched taut around his biceps, support that statement.

It's almost painful to drag my eyes away.

"Okay," I hear myself agree. "I'll call you next time."

We go our separate ways. Darwin heads toward the arcade games he was repairing, and I make a beeline for the one working bathroom. I finished cleaning it last night, but the room is still giving *strong* truck-stop vibes. It's going to need a fresh coat of paint, and maybe new flooring, before it's presentable for the public.

It's saying a lot that the moment the door closes behind me, I feel like I can breathe again. Bracing my hands on the chipped porcelain sink, I glare at my reflection in the mirror.

"You don't like him," I hiss, as if Darwin is going to be standing with his ear pressed to the door. "You don't think he's cute, or like it when he compliments you, or want anything to do with him outside this building."

The Savvy in the mirror doesn't seem to be convinced.

CHAPTER 7
DARWIN

TOUCHED HER.

I put my hands on Savvy's skin, in her hair, on her face, and nothing happened.

Well, *something* happened, but it wasn't the grotesque reaction that my disorder has trained me to associate with skin-to-skin contact.

What's truly remarkable is that I didn't realize what I was doing until after the fact. My panic for her safety eclipsed every other thought in my mind, compulsive, antisocial, or otherwise. Then, when it was all over and I felt confident she was only moderately downplaying her injuries, it hit me.

I touched her, and all it felt was good.

It's one thing to know, objectively, that your mind is playing tricks on you, but it's a whole other to have evidence of it. That's what I've been doing all week at Galactic Guild, *showing* myself that the things I fear are lies. It's a slow, exhausting process, but there *is* progress. Today proved it, because I haven't felt another person's skin against mine in years—*nine*, to be precise—and I didn't fall to pieces.

During the periods when my mental health was at its best, my therapist encouraged me to "get out there." Apparently, even to a licensed psychologist, my being totally disinterested in a relationship was not possible.

There were times when I considered it, but just the thought of dating seemed impossible. Most people my age have been married, they've had kids and traveled and found friends… What would I say to a well-adjusted, normal woman sitting across the table from me? How could I possibly divulge to a near stranger just how limited I am or the terrible partner I would make?

Shame crowds my throat, and it's an effort to keep my eyes on the machine I'm repairing when they seem to drift so easily to Savvy.

She's standing across the room, focused on the new prices she's painting on the big board behind the register. There are tiny specks of white all over her face and her hair is tied up in a messy bun, but she's somehow still adorable and sexy all at once.

Sexy.

Fuck. I have no right to think of her that way, but the memory of her warm, soft skin beneath my fingers makes it ten times harder not to. It's an embarrassing, ridiculous position to find myself in. Me, a forty-five-year-old man, getting worked up over touching a woman's arms, face, and hair while checking for injuries from an overturned game-show wheel.

Not just any woman, either.

So much time has passed, she's so different and so am I, but that doesn't change the fact that Savvy is practically my niece. I'd known Stone since childhood. He was my friend— my *only* friend—and I'm panting after his little girl when he's barely cold in the ground.

I should feel guilty, should be disgusted with myself, but with every brief glimpse I get at the person she's become, I care a little less. Meanwhile, Savvy is clearly committed to ensuring those glimpses are as far and few between as possible. She's so guarded with me, constantly bracing for an emotional blow, and it's not a mystery why.

I should have cleared the air that day she came to my house, or when I showed up here and told her I wanted to help. If I had… Well, I'd still feel guilty. God knows what happened nine years ago isn't the only reason nothing will ever happen.

In the back of my mind, though, I know why I didn't.

I needed to keep a wall between us, but the joke's on me because now all I can think about is the best way to kick it down.

Maybe it would be easier to get past this attraction if it were just physical, but it's not. Her reappearance in my life has made me feel… off kilter. The organ in my chest, that I once believed to be purely functional, seems to be making itself known more and more readily.

Then there's the fact my cock is now hard about three quarters of my waking hours, which is painful on top of inconvenient.

The wrench I'm using to re-tighten the bolts on the side panel of this game slips and clatters off. I turn to reach for it, and, like they're magnetized, my eyes move to Savvy.

She's painting a higher place on the board now, her lips pursed in concentration.

Her T-shirt, the same one with the cut-out sleeves she was wearing the other day, lifts away from her skin when she reaches up, and I catch another glimpse of black ink.

The tattoo. It's none of my business what she thought was important enough to get permanently etched on her skin. So why can't I stop thinking about it?

Irrationally irritated, I turn my eyes back to where they belong. I'm fucking losing it. None of this situation is logical, or ordered, or controlled, and I have no experience in this shit.

This *thing* hanging over our heads has become unbearable.

What would happen if I walked up to her and ripped off the proverbial band aid right now? Would it make things more uncomfortable when she's beginning to relax around me? Maybe this is a time thing, and I just need to fight through this awkward period so we can get to… What? What do I think is going to happen here?

It seems dangerous to even consider.

A knock on the glass front door has me looking automatically to Savvy again. She's frowning at me. "Are you expecting a delivery or something?"

I shake my head. "Stay there, I'll get it."

She doesn't listen, of course, and lingers at my side as I unlock the paper-covered door and pull it open.

After spending so long in the dim lighting of Galactic Guild, it's disorienting to step into bright afternoon sunlight, and I blink down at three of the teenagers from the other day, standing just outside.

"Hi," chirps the girl with the dark hair and ear piercings, beaming at us.

I glance at Savvy, who looks just as bemused as I am. "Uh, hi. We're not open yet."

She isn't put off. "Oh, we know. We're here to help."

"I'm sorry, we're not hiring yet. I'll post something online when we start, but it'll be at least another few weeks," Savvy explains, and I step back, allowing her to take the lead on this.

"You don't have to pay us!" interjects one boy, his eyes widening. "We just thought that if you had some more help, you could reopen sooner." The other boy in the group elbows him, and he grins sheepishly. "Okay, maybe some free laser tag too. But that's not a deal breaker!"

"Shut up about the laser tag, Luke. We're here to help," scolds the girl.

I bite back a smile. It's unusual for me to form an opinion after such a brief interaction, but I'm finding I like them. "What are your names?"

"I'm Marley," says the girl. "This is Luke, and that's King."

Luke, who is blonde, almost as tall as I am, and dressed in a bright-purple anime T-shirt, beams. "We love your books, Mr. Wilder. It's so cool you live in the same town as us. Marley writes a ton of fan fiction for them, but they're not exactly family friendly"—he drops his voice conspiratorially—"if you know what I mean."

"Oh my god, Luke!" squawks Marley as she slaps her hands over her bright-red face, and I'm actively trying not to laugh now.

King, undoubtedly sensing he won't be getting much help from his friends, chips in, "My dad is a contractor, so I know how to fix stuff."

A compelling sales pitch, but Savvy still looks unconvinced. "Listen, it's really sweet of you guys to offer, but we'd need to talk about it."

"You should be made aware that I'm from a *super* poor family. We buy some of my clothes at the thrift store and everything," Marley adds cheerfully. "In case you want to look at it as mentoring underprivileged youth instead of exploiting teenagers for free labor."

Savvy snorts, and I sigh. "Give us five minutes."

The moment the door closes, I turn to face Savvy. "Okay. We need to hire them. If only for the entertainment value."

Her hands move to her hips. "*You* want a group of nerdy sixteen-year-olds running around here, Dar?"

I love it when she calls me that.

Grinning, I cross my arms. "I think you'll remember that *you* were a nerdy sixteen-year-old once. They don't need to do anything big, but if we get some extra help with the cleaning, they'll get their DnD hang-out spot back sooner. We'll need to hire help soon anyway." It seems ominous that even the reminder I knew her when she was sixteen doesn't make me want to end this conversation.

Savvy's eyes sparkle, and her lips curl into a teasing smile. "I wasn't as nerdy as you were."

"Yes, you were."

"Not the point."

Something tightens low in my abdomen as it occurs to me how close we're standing. Is it nearer than platonic business partners would? It *feels* close. I could reach out and touch her again, just like I did before.

My heart jolts.

With difficulty, I swallow. "If you're uncomfortable with it, of course, we'll tell them no. I trust your judgment."

Something behind Savvy's eyes flickers, and whatever warmth was kindling between us is gone so quickly, I'm left questioning whether it was there at all.

She turns away, heading back for the paint. "Sure thing. It's fine, Darwin. Tell them whatever," she tells me over her shoulder.

Wonderful. I'm *Darwin* again. Never before have I disliked the sound of my own name.

I want to argue with her, want to demand she tell me what she's thinking, what she wants… I would do it—would do *anything*—if it meant I could step back in time just a few seconds.

The kids are still waiting outside, and all three look up hopefully. Once again, I glance at Savvy, but she doesn't lift her attention from the board.

I clear my throat. "Why don't you come back on Monday, and we'll have some stuff for you to do. You'll get paid. I'm not using teenagers for free labor."

They're pleased, but I only half hear the rush of thank-yous and hell-yeahs as they wander off; my mind is on the woman behind me.

When the door closes, I find Savvy kneeling on the back counter again, and my mouth goes dry when she pushes up on her knees to reach a higher spot.

For fuck's sake. Does she own a pair of shorts that *aren't* made of skin-tight material? If I can't stop looking at her ass, that means other men sure as hell are too. There seems little point in denying that pisses me off when the possibility alone makes my blood pressure skyrocket.

There's plenty for me to do, but I still linger awkwardly by the front desk, scrambling for a reason to talk to her again. I check my watch. "Are you hungry? I was going to order something for lunch."

She doesn't turn. "I'm good. Thanks, though."

"Are you sure? I thought I'd get a Reuben." It sounds like an offhand comment, but is really more of a desperate plea. Savvy *loves* Reubens, or at least, she used to.

Watching her as closely as I am, I catch the tiny pause. "That's okay."

Fuck, this is unbearable. Is this how other people feel when they're forced to communicate with me?

Defeated, I turn back toward the arcade. Movement in the corner of my vision makes me turn, though, and my heart shoots into my throat.

"Holy fuck!" I stumble backward, hitting the back of my legs on the front desk and—dignity forgotten—clamber up onto the surface.

"What?" comes Savvy's alarmed voice. Wordlessly, I point toward the hall leading to the bathrooms. Twenty feet away from us, a fucking *rat* is wandering into the room, sniffing at the contractor trash bags Savvy stuffed with torn-up carpeting.

I know the moment she sees it, because there's an startled gasp behind me.

This situation is preposterous. I'm standing on the furniture to get away from an animal that would likely run off if I approached it, but I can't help it. My skin is crawling, and my back is damp with sweat. Have I ever seen a rat before? In person? If I have, I don't remember.

"What do we do?" asks Savvy, her voice high with panic. At least I'm not alone here. She's standing on the narrow strip of counter that lines the wall behind the desk, wide eyed and clutching her hands to her chest.

Ideally, this would be the moment where I save the day and impress her with my stoicism in the face of a vermin infestation. Unfortunately, I'm paralyzed, too busy trying to recall the articles I've read about rat-borne pathogens to impress anyone.

What if that thing has been walking around on the floor where I was sitting a few minutes ago?

Have I touched rat shit? My stomach rolls.

A white sneaker appears on the desk beside me, and I thankfully have enough sanity left to turn and offer Savvy my hand, helping her over the four-foot gap between the desk and counter. "Holy crap," she mumbles, her back brushing my chest as she inches to the edge for a clearer view. "It's *huge.*"

The rat trots farther into the room, unaware or uncaring that its appearance has caused turmoil amongst Galactic Guild's human inhabitants. Instinctively, I grab Savvy's shoulders, dragging her back from the edge of the desk.

"Do we run for it?" I look toward the door. The rat is closer. Are they fast?

Savvy shakes her head. "All my stuff is over there! Oh my god, I'm going to puke."

Yeah, that makes two of us.

Stooping down, I grab the wireless mouse. "I'm going to try to scare it," I tell her with more confidence than I feel, then chuck it at the wall above the rat's head. The device shatters, sending bits of plastic everywhere, but the animal doesn't seem bothered.

Savvy tries too, throwing a cup of pens that scatter over the floor.

"What kind of rat doesn't get scared by that?" she wails,

looking up at me in horror when this attempt garners no more success. "Wouldn't you be disturbed by a metal cup the size of your body being hurled at you?"

"It's probably used to the noise." I shudder. "That, or it's gone mad from nutritional deficiency after living off those frozen pizzas Stone stocked."

"So, we have a super rat?"

"It appears so."

We fall silent, still crowded together on the center of the desk, watching the rat move over to where Savvy's backpack is sitting on the floor beside the snack bar. "Oh, that little asshole," she hisses when it pokes its head in through the open zipper.

A quick scan of the area confirms there seems to be little that could be helpful. "Does animal control respond to calls about rodents?"

Savvy whips around, eyes huge. "Rodents? As in *plural*? You think there are *more*?"

It seems likely, but it won't do us any good to dwell on that now. "I doubt it," I lie instead, offering her a reassuring smile. "There was something in a nature magazine I subscribe to about large male rats not allowing others in their territory."

"You are so full of shit, Darwin Wilder." But there's no genuine anger in her voice. Suddenly, the preposterous predicament we've found ourselves in doesn't seem so bad.

For one thing, we're so close that I can smell the fruity gum she likes to chew on her breath and the clean scent of shampoo in her hair.

For another, I touched her. Again.

Come to think of it, the super rat can take his damn time.

Savvy obviously feels differently. Edging to the other side of the desk, she peeks down. I watch as she gets to her knees and reaches over to grab a plastic trash can. "It's not going to care if we throw trash at it," I caution as she removes the mostly empty plastic lining.

"Yeah, I don't either." She looks over her shoulder at me. "Promise to avenge me should this go wrong?"

"I—what?"

Before I can say another word or make a move to stop her, Savvy jumps off the desk with the trash bin held under her arm. The rat is still sniffing around in her backpack, its long, worm-like tail poking out from beside the zipper.

"Savvy! Don't go near it!" I snarl. When it becomes clear she isn't going to stop, I jump off the desk too. I've only made it halfway across the room, however, before Savvy turns the waste basket over and slams it down right over the backpack and rat with a hollow *thud*, trapping both inside.

We're both silent for a long moment, staring at it. Finally, Savvy looks back at me, eyes wide. "What now?"

I pull my phone from my pocket, shaking my head. "We're calling a fucking exterminator."

To Do: ☆

~~Find a realtor for CC~~

~~Meeting with accountant~~
~~Find an accountant~~

Exact revenge on Caleb

Clean literally everything

Fix literally everything

~~Talk to HIM~~

~~New Vacuum~~

Rip up stained carpet in lobby+snackbar

Replace those long lightbulbs in the ceiling

Find out which games in arcade don't work

Fix roof leak

Reconnect security system (at some point)

Find a therapist

Figure out why my car is making that clanky noise

CHAPTER 8
SAVVY

MY FATHER'S ashes are sitting beside my breakfast.

Somehow, despite finding the cremation service, signing lots of paperwork, and being his only child, it never occurred to me that I'd be the one responsible for *doing something* with them.

My grandparents have been dead since before I was born, and my mother is too busy trying to save her marriage to her third husband to care about the remains of the first. Darwin is the only person I could ask about this, and inviting any kind of emotional connection between us seems like a bad idea.

What do you do with the ashes of someone who was, in life, a good if absent-minded father, and in death, a man who might have ruined your life?

Google didn't have an answer, and my Reddit post was flagged, so I'm on my own. It's been over a month since I got his remains back from the funeral home, and I still don't have any idea. He's just... sitting there. Right next to a pile of unopened bills and my birth control prescription.

Living alone in my childhood home, with only Dad's ashes for company, feels like I've fallen through a wormhole into a parallel dimension. Everything is familiar, but it still doesn't feel quite real.

Maybe, it's because everything happened so fast. When he was first diagnosed and began treatment, I could make the drive from the city where I was living with my ex back to the hospital whenever he needed me. His health deteriorated fast, though, and before I knew it, I was back at home, shuffling Dad to and from chemo appointments in between rideshare shifts.

We spent a lot of time together in waiting rooms, and later when he was admitted to the hospital. We talked about a lot, too, but it hadn't occurred to him to mention the state of his business. Any time I brought up Galactic

Guild, he insisted he had a "great manager" in place and that I didn't need to worry about it.

I was stressed, exhausted, and sad about being dumped by my boyfriend of six months who wasn't "really into the long distance thing." Accepting what Dad was telling me— even if there were a few red flags waving around in the back of my mind—was easier than adding another massive responsibility to my plate.

In a predictable turn of events, burying my head in the sand didn't turn out well. Dad's "great manager" was a guy named Ted (last name unknown), and the only thing he was great at was doing as little work as possible. Do I wish I'd investigated the situation sooner? Of course. It wouldn't have made much difference in the financial situation, but maybe I wouldn't be spending my entire weekend working. *With Dar.*

I'm working to fix up Galactic Guild with Darwin.

Darwin is helping me fix Galactic Guild.

Repair and cleaning assistance provided by Darwin Wilder, best-selling author with a penchant for gagging when confronted with dirt.

Yeah, it doesn't matter how often I say it. It's still weird.

Heaving a sigh, I gather up my breakfast plate and pad to

the kitchen sink. It's kind of grim to stack my dishes atop three meals' worth of plates and cutlery from yesterday, yet still not have enough to justify running the dishwasher. Then again, everything about this room is pretty depressing.

I'm living in a tomb, complete with human remains and all Dad's worldly possessions.

Leaning back against the countertop, I survey the room. It's almost exactly the same as it was when I was growing up and spending every other weekend here. Everything from the dark wooden cabinets to faded magnets on the fridge. A hand-drawn Father's Day card is tacked to the wall beside an old landline that hasn't been connected for years.

It's mine now.

My useless brick phone. My chipped tile. My sky-high mortgage payment.

Do I want to live in the same aging, split-level suburban hellscape that I grew up in? No, but I'm going to be here for a while, and it wouldn't hurt to clean this place up a little. Maybe I'd feel less dread coming home every night if I got rid of Dad's old video game collection and the rows of collectable figurines—still preserved in their boxes—sitting on shelves above the couch.

My heart is heavy as I push off the counter and begin gathering my things to go. The search for my phone (which occurs at least three times a day) takes longer than normal, so by the time I make it to my car, I'm already running late.

My plan was to hit the hardware store before Galactic Guild, but all plans evaporate when I turn my key in the ignition and… *nothing*.

I try again, because maybe today will be the first time in my entire life that I get lucky and my car will magically recover from whatever ails it.

It doesn't.

Hands shaking and eyes burning, I shove the door back open and stumble out onto the driveway.

"Are. You. Fucking. Kidding. Me?" I punctuate each word with a kick against the tire.

Was I a hostile dictator in a past life or something? Because the amount of *bullshit* raining down on me is starting to feel really personal. I know for a fact I haven't done anything to deserve such an extreme dose of karmic justice.

Panting, I lean back against the heap of junk and stare up at the sky, weighing my options. I could call a rideshare or a cab. Or, I could stab myself in the eye with a fork and eat my weight in chocolate pudding at the hospital instead of deciding anything.

All are viable options, but my bank account really isn't in any state to afford such luxuries, especially with an unexpected car repair bill coming.

There's one other choice, but calling him feels… personal. You call friends or family for a ride. Darwin is my father's best friend, the man who broke my heart and, more recently, my reluctant business partner (also the star in some very graphic dreams which I'm pretending didn't happen).

Despite the conversation we had the other day after he rescued me from the wheel, I never intended to actually call him for anything. We're not friends. Asking for his help and inviting him into my life outside Galactic Guild, feels like it would cross the unspoken boundary we've drawn. *I've drawn.*

Boundaries are important here. It's so easy to be around him that I find myself scrambling to keep it together about a dozen times a day. For me, loving Darwin Wilder is muscle memory, like riding a bike or dancing to your favorite song. It just *happens*, and I need to make sure it *doesn't*.

I press my hands over my face, trying to think through the self-pity and panic clouding my mind. Am I being ridiculous? Probably. Why should I pay twenty dollars for a cab when my house is barely out of the way for Darwin? We're going to the same place. It doesn't have to be a big deal.

I pull out my phone and find the contact I haven't used for nine years, but never deleted.

————

I'm a little surprised by how quickly Dar's expensive electric car pulls into the driveway. It's not even fifteen minutes later, and when I called him, he said he was at home. Which means he must have jumped in the car the moment we hung up.

Darwin steps out before I can even make it off the front stoop, brow furrowed.

The man is wearing a black T-shirt today—a *tight* black t-shirt—and it's all I can do to stop myself from cursing out the universe for the second time in one morning. *God actual fucking damnit.* Even seventy-year-old Mrs. Paul from next door has stopped sweeping pine needles off her walkway to check him out.

He's a science-fiction author. Aren't they supposed to be skinny and weird smelling? Couldn't he have had a weird mole on his chin or fart when he laughs?

"Hi." I arrange my face into something (hopefully) resembling a grateful smile. "Thanks for this."

"Is it the battery?" asks Darwin, already circling the hood of my car in problem-solving mode.

"Maybe." I pull the elastic off my wrist and gather my hair into a messy bun. The roots are beginning to show, but a trip to the salon is definitely not in the cards now. "I'll deal with it later. I just figured since you were driving to Galactic Guild anyway and this is sort of on the way—"

Darwin's sharp look puts an end to my rambling. "I'm happy to help. Would you rather we try to jump it now or tonight after I drop you off?"

We.

My stomach rolls, but I stand straighter, glaring at him. "I'm not helpless, Darwin. This is just... It happens! I didn't do anything to cause this. Cars break down! I'm an adult. It's nothing I can't handle." I sound like a lunatic, stumbling over my words in my rush to get them out.

God, I'm so stupid. The last few weeks, when it's been just the two of us alone at Galactic Guild, it's felt good. *Easy.* So easy that, despite my resolve not to, I've allowed myself to relax around him. Then, with the whole giant wheel thing and our narrow escape from super rat... I allowed myself to believe Dar doesn't see me as a giant, bumbling idiot.

Even with a lifetime of fuckups behind me, I'm not sure I've ever felt so ashamed of myself. This man thinks I'm a helpless little fool, fumbling her way through life. *That's* what all this has been about. He is overcoming his disorder because he'd rather be miserable and uncomfortable than sit back and watch me burn Galactic Guild to the ground.

Darwin stares at me, bemused. "I didn't say you *couldn't* handle it, Savvy."

Hah.

Not bothering to respond, I turn, marching around his car to the passenger side. I feel the weight of eyes on me, but I avoid looking back as I yank open the door and plop down onto the cool leather seat, slamming the door behind me a little too hard.

Awesome. Now I look like I'm having a tantrum too.

The interior of this thing is even fancier than it looks from outside. My sneakers are scuffed and dirty, and I wince, thinking of the face he'll make when he realizes I've left dust on his impeccably clean floor mat. The seat under my cheap-shorts-wearing ass is so pristine, it's like no one has ever sat in it before.

Maybe no one has.

I'd hoped that giving myself a few seconds away would help me get my shit together, but I hadn't considered that I would be in a small, enclosed space that smells like him.

My stomach twists as the driver's side opens and Darwin

gets in, folding his long limbs into the tight space with more grace than I managed. Neither of us speak as he presses a button—because why would someone as evolved as Darwin need something as pedestrian as car keys—and backs out of the driveway.

Mrs. Paul is still craning her neck for one last look at him as we pull around the scruffy tree in the center of the cul-de-sac.

He glances at me when we stop at the end of the road. "Savvy—"

"Can we not?" I keep my eyes trained forward. I don't need more half-hearted attempts to keep up the pretense that anyone in this car thinks I'm a competent adult; I'm not. The only thing worse than Darwin thinking it, is for him to pretend he doesn't for my benefit.

He makes a small, frustrated noise. "I was trying to help."

"You *are* helping me." I gesture vaguely around at his fancy car. "I asked for a ride, and you're giving me a ride. Thanks, partner. By the way, do you remember that annual laser tag tournament my dad used to do? I'm thinking we should restart it. Also, did you hear about what they did to poor Pluto? *So* disrespectful."

Darwin isn't distracted. "You're being ridiculous. Are you so proud that you can't let me help jump your car battery?"

I let out a hard, disbelieving laugh. "Yup. I'm super proud. That's exactly right, Darwin. Your deductive reasoning remains top notch. I'll be sure to work on that."

We stop at a red light, and Darwin rounds on me. In the confines of the car, we're almost nose to nose, and something tightens inside me as those dark eyes bore into my own.

"I'll call someone to pick up your car."

Oh my god.

I whip around, my heart beating harder than that time Raven forced me to go running with her. "If you do that, I'm going to pee in your gas tank, you condescending butthole."

"It's electric. There isn't a gas tank to pee in. Also… okay, how would you even do that?"

I cross my arms. "I have my ways, Wilder. Don't test me. And leave my car alone."

He lets out a long hiss, like he's trying to vent the frustration that's built up during this argument. "I don't understand why you won't let me take care of this for you. It's a small thing."

"Oh my god, drop it! It's none of your business!"

He stays silent for all of five seconds. "Will you please just—"

Darwin's next words are drowned out, however, as I open my mouth and start to sing.

CHAPTER 9
SAVVY

"A-SIX."

Dar hisses, glaring at me over the top of his board. "Hit."

"You've been a gamer for how long? How are you still a sore loser?" I giggle, tucking my legs beneath me and holding out my palm. Dar drops a little ship into it.

"I'm not a sore loser, I'm just convinced you're cheating and can't work out how."

"Is this your villain origin story?" "No, but I suspect it's yours."

I burst into laughter, trying to ignore the butterflies that erupt in my belly at our banter. As I watch, Dar shuts his board sourly and gets to his feet, crossing to the pantry and calling over his shoulder, "Can I get you a victory orange soda?"

"Sure!"

This is the kind of stuff that makes it so hard to be objective about my feelings for him. It's not like I'm desperately in love with some teacher who views me as any other student.

Dar and I get along so well—we always have—and now I'm old enough to be more than just his best friend's daughter.

Does he get lonely?

Does he think about me when I'm not here? Does he ever wish I would come back sooner?

There are so many questions that seem unanswerable, and the looming date of my departure for college is like a sword waiting to fall. Somehow, it's become so important that I find out for sure before I leave.

I can't stomach the possibility of my future self getting felt up at some frat party while Dar sits alone in this house hours away, feeling even the tiniest fraction of what I do.

I'm eighteen years old, and I've never even been kissed. How long can I keep this up? What's better: keep pining away from a distance, hoping for a few hours together a few times a year, or to know for sure one way or another?

Swallowing past the lump in my throat, I stand, wiping my sweaty palms on my shorts as Dar re-emerges from the pantry holding a soda for me and a bottled water for himself.

Outside, thunder booms loudly enough to make me jump, cutting through my preoccupation with the man in front of me.

He hands me the drink, frowning distractedly at the rain-streaked windows that line the room. "If this doesn't stop soon, you'll have to spend the night. I don't want you driving in the dark during a storm."

My heart flutters at the thought of seeing him first thing in the morning.

Does he get bedhead? I bet he does, and it's probably adorable. "Another game?" I ask, and my voice sounds higher than usual.

Dar doesn't notice. "I wouldn't dare." He chuckles, leaning back against the kitchen counter and taking a long sip of water.

I take a step closer, a thrill of fear and excitement traveling up my spine. If I took one step, I could take another, so I do. There are only four feet between us now.

"Will you miss me when I'm at college?" My heart pounds against my ribcage as Dar lowers his bottle, gazing at me through the gloomy light.

"You know I will." He sounds annoyed that I even asked.

I didn't know, actually. Not for sure. The man keeps everything so close to the vest; the closest I've ever gotten to a compliment from him was being told four years ago that my new haircut suited me. I remember, because it was the very first time Darwin Wilder gave me butterflies.

Swallowing, I wrap an arm around myself, my hand pressing over the fresh tattoo inked on my ribs.

I take another step, and Dar must realize I have something on my mind. We're close together now. Too close. His expression goes wooden, and he stares at me, unmoving. "Savvy?"

Well… I've come this far.

Reaching out, my hands find his shoulders, warm and solid. Before he can say another word, before I can chicken out and pretend there was just a speck of lint on his shirt, I stand on my toes and press my lips to Dar's.

He doesn't move.

The whole room seems to have gone quiet around us. I can't hear the rain, or the thunder, or anything at all except my own blood rushing in my ears. My sharp inhale sounds unnaturally loud as I pull away, just an inch.

We both stand still, suspended in time, and it feels like my whole life is hanging on this one moment.

Kiss me back. Please kiss me back. He doesn't.

Then, everything seems to turn back on at once.

Dar wrenches himself away from me, so quickly that I stumble forward, catching myself on the countertop. He strides rapidly to the sink in the kitchen island and turns on the water. A quiet cry of horror breaks from my chest as his hand moves under the stream and back to his face—scrubbing my kiss away.

No.

This isn't actually happening, is it? But, even as I ask myself the question, I know it is. I did this. Now, all I can do is watch, frozen to the spot, as he washes and washes, his movements growing more and more shaky. The roughness of his beard is still fresh on my face.

It's not until my vision blurs that I realize I'm crying.

"Dar," I whisper, because I can't take it anymore. I can't watch this.

He ignores me. Not knowing what else to do, I take a step forward, and that movement must break through whatever state I put him in. "Don't."

One word, and something deep inside me shatters.

Dar hits the faucet and leans over, bracing his hands on the counter.

His breathing is ragged. "What were you thinking?"

Tears are streaming down my cheeks now. "I'm sorry," I whisper, pathetic and broken, as if a few words could ever be enough to fix this. "I didn't think—"

"No. You didn't think, Savvy," Dar snarls. To my horror, he makes a rough, gagging noise. Vomit hits the sink as my back hits the table behind me. I hadn't even realized I was moving away.

I can't help him, can't undo the damage my actions have caused. I can just stand here, useless and horrified, with guilt clogging my throat.

Finally, Dar straightens up. His face is chalk white, and it seems like it takes him an inordinate amount of effort just to look at me. "Physical touch isn't something I want or need."

His words slide down my spine like ice, and I want to run away so badly. I don't want to face what I've done, but I have to, because I'm paralyzed as my shattered heart rips me apart from the inside out.

His jaw is tight as he spits, "Why would you do that? Did you think I would welcome it? You're a child. An irresponsible, selfish child, and tonight proves it."

A helpless little noise breaks free from my lips, but I don't reply. How could I?

Dar shakes his head, disgust evident in every strained inch of his body. "You crossed a line, Savvy. Fuck!" His fist comes down on the edge of the counter with a bang that I feel like a physical blow. "Get the fuck out. *Now*. Don't come back. I mean it."

The command unlocks whatever was frozen inside me, and I seize my bag from the table, running for the door. Ripping it open, I pelt out into the rain, my flip-flops slipping in the inches of water running down the driveway, and I fall. The pain of my skinned knee barely registers. Scrambling forward, I lunge for the car door.

"Savvy!" Dar bellows, the powerful volume of his voice cutting over the noise of the pounding rain and my own sobs. "Fuck—come back inside. Don't drive in this!"

I ignore him. I don't look back. I don't stop. My car speeds back, spraying water onto the windows. Before I turn out onto the street, though, I pause, looking back. I can barely see him through the rain, just a blurry silhouette standing on the porch of the big, lonely white house on the hill.

Every bit of this is my fault. Every word he said was the truth. I fucked up. I fucked up so bad, and the least I can do is honor his wishes.

This is the last time I'll ever see Darwin Wilder.

CHAPTER 10
DARWIN

SAVVY SINGS A VERY OFF-KEY rendition of "Bohemian Rhapsody" at the top of her lungs for the entire fifteen-minute drive to Galactic Guild.

As we pull into the parking lot, there's no sign of it stopping. I'm becoming concerned the torture will continue when we go inside. Thankfully, there are families heading into classes at the neighboring karate place. She must care what other people think, because the Galileos stop the moment I open my car door.

I've managed to piss her off before we've even entered the building.

Not a promising start to the day.

Last night, laying in bed, I felt calm for the first time in… forever. My thoughts weren't racing, my pulse was even, and I realized I hadn't had an obsessive episode in days. Normally, overcoming my insomnia requires two prescription medications, total darkness, a white noise machine, and a blessing from the Pope.

This morning, I woke up with my e-reader resting on my

chest, the bedroom lights still on, and sunlight streaming in through the window. I'd slept a full ten hours, and didn't wake up once.

The only thing more disconcerting than that was the erection throbbing against my stomach. I'm a healthy adult male; morning wood happens. Ordinarily, I ignore it or jerk off purely to relieve the ache. My mind is on what I'm going to make for breakfast, what I'll write that day, or whatever daily task I happen to be dreading.

It's not about giving myself pleasure.

I certainly never conjure up fantasies that are so well formed and vivid, it's as though they've been developing just below the surface of my consciousness, waiting for their opportunity to rise.

But that's what happened this time.

Without stopping to think about it, my hand had drifted down, gripping myself through the cotton of my sweatpants. I groaned, my eyes shutting. No sooner had my hand pushed beneath the waistband to grasp my bare cock than a quiet, sweet female voice was whispering in my ear.

"Can I touch you, Dar?" Savvy curled closer, her breasts pushing against my side.

I tried to dismiss the fantasy, to clear my mind. With every stroke it only became more clear, though, and it felt too goddamn good to stop. Weeks of seeing her in those cock-tease shorts, of catching her familiar scent in the air around Galactic Guild, of *fucking touching her*, brought me to the brink. Suddenly, I was more turned on than I'd ever been in my life, and I didn't want it to end.

Sleep-tousled pink hair fell around her shoulders as she sat up, straddling my thigh while dressed only in a thin white tank top and panties with little cherries printed on them. Her lips parted as she gazed down at me, tracing her hands over my bare abdomen and down to where my dick was tenting my sweatpants.

"Please, Dar?" she begged, and I could feel the heat from her pussy even through two layers of fabric. "I need it so bad."

Savvy moaned as I reached down to release my cock, and leaned forward to kiss my chest as a hand that was smaller and softer than my own found my length.

I let her play, let her stroke me gently, teasingly, as the sound of our ragged breathing replaced the quiet of the room.

"How's that?" she murmured, blinking down at me from beneath heavy lids. I knew what she wanted, knew what she's asking for.

My hands found her ass, squeezing. "I'd like your hot little cunt better." Bedding rustled as she crawled over me, and I could barely breathe from how badly I wanted to be inside her. "Hurry." My voice was rough, desperate, and Savvy moaned, tugging her panties to the side and—

I came. So hard that my entire body shook from the intensity of it. Even after I'd fallen back into my pillows, panting, it was difficult to process what just happened.

I'd masturbated to thoughts of Savvy. It was surreal, and even as minutes passed and my cum began to cool on my skin, I still couldn't quite wrap my head around it.

Sex has always been off the table for me. Always. My obsessions began to be a real problem during puberty, and, while Stone was panting after every girl who might be interested in him, I was struggling to cover up my escalating intrusive thoughts. Then, as I got older, even when my mental health was at its best and I went weeks without a single episode, I still wasn't interested.

I've barely tolerated being touched by another person, never mind… that. I couldn't even fantasize about someone putting their hands on me without my skin crawling and dread expanding painfully in my chest. While I could appreciate a woman's beauty, like any other red-blooded, heterosexual man, it's always stopped there.

Or it *did* stop there, until I jerked off to fantasies of my dead best friend's daughter.

The worst part was that as I laid there, covered in my own release, I wasn't even surprised. Savvy has gotten under my skin in a way no one ever has, and it seems perfectly ironic that I'm having my sexual awakening several decades late for the most inappropriate woman on the planet.

A woman whom I seem to push further away every time I open my mouth, because we've been tiptoeing around the real problem, pretending it didn't happen to save ourselves from embarrassment.

It needs to end.

This morning, I was having my first truly productive writing session in the better part of a year. The moment Savvy's name came up on my phone, however, I all but threw myself over the desk to answer it, spilling coffee everywhere.

It's pointless to pretend this hasn't gotten wildly out of hand.

There's no way she's interested. Not anymore. Savvy is... she's fucking incredible. I've never met someone so brave, so incredibly strong even with the weight of Stone's choices on her shoulders. That *on top of* being the most effortlessly, mind-numbingly beautiful woman I've ever seen. How much of a draw could a man like me, with the limitations I have, be for her? I might not have a shot here, but these feelings are my problem to sort out. Hell, maybe I deserve to have my heart broken after all I've done, but I can't use something that hurts her as a shield to protect myself anymore. It's not fair, and I can't stand the thought of her walking around feeling less about herself because of me.

This ends now.

"Savvy," I say when the door to Galactic Guild shuts quietly behind me. My partner is already pacing across the lobby to the snack bar, pretending she didn't hear me.

I follow, guilt and shame twisting bitterly inside me. She

always knows the right things to say, senses when I'm on edge and exactly how to distract me. Meanwhile, I seem to make misstep after misstep, blundering my way through this relationship like a bull in a china shop.

Professional relationship. Not… not the other kind.

It's becoming more difficult to silence that not-so-tiny part of me that desperately wants it to be *the other kind*.

"I just want to get this done and go home, Darwin," she says over her shoulder, and there's a weariness in her voice that I'm not sure I've ever heard there before.

"I just want to talk about what happened nine years ago."

Savvy stills, the pen she just picked up going slack in her hand. Slowly, she turns to face me, folding her arms over her chest and shrinking in on herself before my eyes. Does she think I'm going to blame her?

My stomach twists, and I force myself to take a deep breath, attempting to calm my racing pulse. "What I said to you that day was a reflection of my own issues. There's no excuse for it. Nor is there an excuse for me waiting nine years to apologize to you. I believed it would clear my conscience, but do nothing for you. I see now that was wrong." Swallowing against the tightness in my throat, I continue, not letting myself look away. "I'm sorry. Truly sorry. For all of it."

She lowers her eyes to the floor. "It's… nice of you to say that, Dar, but I think it's pretty obvious you were right."

Her words hit me right in the chest, knocking the air from my lungs. "No. *No*, Savvy," I protest, horror and guilt clawing viciously inside me. "No, I wasn't right. It wasn't what I thought then, and it isn't what I think now. It's—*fuck*—it's the opposite. I'm in awe of you, and I always have been. I've never known someone who charges so fearlessly into life, even when she might get hurt. It's who I wish I was, what I wish I could do."

Her eyes are shining with tears now. She looks so small, so vulnerable, that there's nothing I want more than to cross the five feet between us and pull her into my arms. Never in my life has hugging someone felt natural, but now, with her, it feels unnatural *not to.*

"I was so stupid," she whispers, and as the first tear falls, I've never loathed myself more. "I had a crush on you for *years*. It was just one of those things, you know? Then we were spending all that time together, and I built it up in my head, making it more than it was."

Yeah. I do know. The universe has been evening the score.

"You were brave," I tell her, my voice rough. "If I was… If I was normal, I would have handled it better."

Savvy's eyes, still wet with tears, flash. "Don't talk about yourself like that."

My chest feels like it's going to cave in. "How do you think I feel when I hear you call yourself stupid? Or a mess?"

We both fall silent, staring at each other.

"I never allowed someone close enough to touch me the way you did that day." My smile is bitter, and I almost relish the embarrassment that comes from admitting this to her. I deserve to feel just as awful as I made Savvy feel that day. "I'm not proud of it. My disorder wasn't under control until recently, it took a long time… It doesn't matter. I don't want to bore you. My point is that I would have lashed out at anyone in that situation."

Savvy sniffs. "I'm so sorry, Dar."

"I am too."

Just like the other day when we stood together on the desk, or before that when I saved her from the wheel, touching her isn't a conscious decision.

I lurch forward, and Savvy barely has time to squeak in surprise before I'm wrapping her in my arms, holding her so close that the warmth from her body bleeds into mine and the scent of her makes my head go fuzzy.

There's no ignoring how perfectly she fits against me, or the way it makes me feel when the tension in her muscles slowly fades and her arms snake around my waist, holding me as tightly as I'm holding her.

This is… this is a fucking *hug*.

I'm hugging Savvy, and there's not enough room for the range of emotions erupting inside me.

She clings to me, and I have grit my teeth to keep myself from breaking down too when her body begins to shake with silent sobs. Her face is buried in my chest, and I can feel the wet heat of her tears soaking through my shirt, but I don't care.

For once, the gnawing fear that's existed at the edge of my mind for as long as I can remember is nowhere to be found. Even through the pain and regret, I'm *holding* her. We're holding each other, and it doesn't feel anything but right.

I might be a coward, but she makes me want to be brave.

Without thinking, I press my lips to her temple and speak in a quiet rush in her ear. "None of this is ideal, and I'm furious with Stone for the state he left things, but you're not rolling over and taking the shitty card you were dealt. You're here every day, fighting and trying to make this place better. I trust you completely. I know you're going to do this, and I'll be here to support you every step of the way. As long as you need me."

Never before have I prayed or asked the universe for favors, but I do now. If I've ever done anything good in my life to tip the scales in my favor, *please let her need me.*

Savvy doesn't respond, but burrows closer, her hands pressed flat to my back.

I never want this to end—could happily stand here holding her for hours—but too soon, Savvy's arms relax. Reluctantly, I lean away to see her face, and the look of vulnerable, raw hope that I see there burns through me.

She wipes her eyes. "I was so stupid to do that. Stupid not to realize you aren't interested. Stupid not to realize you don't want… you know."

My head tilts to the side as I turn her words over in my mind. *Aren't* interested, not *weren't* interested. It's a subtle distinction, but I seize upon it like a drowning man. She's thought about this recently, and, whether she realizes it or not, my little tornado just showed her hand.

She wants me.

How do I know I can actually do this, though? I'm too fucking old for her, and just because my obsessions have improved doesn't mean they'll stay that way. The episode before she came back into my life is proof of how quickly it can all go to hell. I have no way of knowing for sure if the way I'm feeling or the things I want from her are all in my head.

What if I try to kiss her and gag? What if I press my hand between her thighs and feel the wetness she's made for me, then wrench away to scrub my skin raw? I couldn't live with myself if I hurt her again, if I gave her hope and snatched it back.

There's so much against us. So many reasons not to try.

"I'm not in the same place I was then. Therapy has helped. I'm medicated. Things got bad after my series ended, and Stone…" I push past the sick twist of guilt at the sound of my old friend's name. "Being here and helping you with Galactic Guild is the closest I've ever felt to *normal*. My mind feels like my own."

Savvy looks at me, and I can see her wondering, can see that tiny flicker of hope behind her eyes. "I've thought you hated me for so long." She lets out a watery, miserable laugh. "I've been acting so crazy."

"I can hardly blame you."

"Still." She makes a face. "Sometimes it feels like I mess up everything I touch."

Everything feels like a mess right now. The pair of us are caught in a tangled web of pain and regret, past and present, assumptions and misunderstandings. Does any of it matter anymore? Really?

I swallow around my heart, which is suddenly lodged in my throat. "What if we start fresh? Right now."

Savvy's eyebrows pull together, and she leans back against the snack bar. "What, you mean just… let it all go?"

"Yes. From today on, it's just you and me, figuring it out as we go. Partners."

The world seems to slow as the words hang in the air between us. She could say no. I try to prepare myself for that. Maybe she'll feel there's too much history. Maybe I've hurt her too badly. Maybe—

"Okay." Savvy holds out her hand, her soft smile letting me know she's remembering how I offered the same thing our very first night here. "Partners."

We both pause when I reach out, staring at my ungloved hand inches from hers. The skin isn't angry and red like it was the day she came to my house, but it's impossible to miss the rough spots and healing cracks, evidence of just how far gone I'd been only a few weeks ago.

I've touched her since then, multiple times, and her tears drying on my shirt are proof. Still, this feels different. *Deliberate.*

"You don't have to if you don't want to," Savvy says, her voice almost unbearably understanding. "I'll accept a verbal agreement." She smiles gently, showing she means it.

This feels important, though, the first true test of what I've been thinking—*feeling*. If I can touch her, skin to skin, and not just as some kind of instinctual reaction… I don't allow myself to think further than that.

Another heartbeat, then two, and I take her hand in mine.

There are a lot of things I feel as we stand there holding on to each other, but none of them are bad.

"Partners," I agree.

When our hands fall back to our sides, Savvy bites her lip,

obviously apprehensive. "Can I ask you something? It's kind of a favor."

My answer comes quickly. "Anything."

I mean it. Does she want a sports car? A back rub? The moon? Whatever the case, I'll make it happen. This woman has me wrapped around her little finger, and I doubt she has the slightest idea.

"My dad's ashes."

Not what I was expecting, but okay. "What about them?"

She winces. "I don't know what to do with them. He's been sitting on the kitchen table for over a month. Not a great eternal resting place. I'm mad at him, don't get me wrong, but he was still my dad."

"I… have an idea, actually. For something he would like." I rub the back of my neck. "Let me see if it's possible before I run it by you."

Savvy shakes her head. "You don't need to run it by me. I…" Her gaze lifts to mine. "I trust you."

To Do: ☆

~~Find a realtor for GG~~

~~Meeting with accountant~~

~~Find an accountant~~

Exact revenge on Caleb

Clean literally everything

Fix literally everything

~~Talk to HIM~~

~~New Vacuum~~

~~Rip up stained carpet in lobby+snackbar~~

~~Replace those long lightbulbs in the ceiling~~

~~Find out which games in arcade don't~~ work

~~Fix roof leak~~

~~Reconnect security system (at some point)~~

Find a therapist

~~Figure out why my car is making that clanky noise~~

New bathroom light fixture

~~Research competitor pricing~~

Complete the Google Ads course

Locate source of weird smell in back hallway

Buy tampons!!!!!!!!

CHAPTER 11
SAVVY

"OKAY, SHOW ME AGAIN."

To his credit, Dar doesn't seem annoyed. I wouldn't blame him if he was. This is the third time in an hour he's explained how to work the new security system, and the third time in an hour I've set it off by opening a door.

"You're younger than me." He grins, moving around the back of Dad's old desk where I'm stationed, squinting at the computer screen. "Shouldn't you be the more technologically literate of the two of us?"

I sigh noisily, attempting not to enjoy the way he leans over my chair, trapping me between his arms.

In my defense, they're very good arms. Muscular without being buff, and dusted with just the right amount of dark hair. Even his hands, which look so much better than they did only a week ago, are so freaking *masculine*.

Now that I think about it, the arms might be a big part of why I still haven't figured this software out.

"See here?" Dar explains patiently, opening the home screen. "There are three settings, one for when we're open and people are here, which will only go off if there's a fire or someone uses the emergency doors. The second is for when we're closed, but you or other employees are here, which arms the doors and windows. The third is for when the building is empty, which detects fire or motion of any kind. Looks like you've been setting three instead of two."

I nod, staring at the screen where Dar is clicking through the steps, trying to focus. His chest brushes my shoulder, and I lean back just a little, pressing myself up against him in the tiniest, most innocent way.

We both pretend not to notice.

It's been a week since we cleared the air and agreed to start fresh, and while it seems ridiculous to be so bent out of shape over a handshake and a hug, I can't stop thinking about it. Somehow, I've gone from a modern, sex- positive woman to a Victorian lady-in-waiting, getting all aflutter over Dar's hand brushing mine.

At least I got to keep the modern accessories. There's no way I could get through this without a vibrator. Or two.

Okay, sue me, there are four.

"What's your code?" Feeling the low rumble of his voice against my back is very distracting.

"Um." My eyelids flutter, and I'm grateful he can't see my face… Or tell that my panties are now soaked from the most chaste, minimal physical contact possible. "You told me not to tell anyone my code."

Dar huffs, his warm breath ghosting over my ear. "Don't you trust me?"

"Oh, I definitely trust you. Which is why I'm listening to your very sensible advice not to tell anyone my code." I giggle, leaning over so I can see his playfully put-upon expression.

"I'm not going to rob myself, Savvy." He sounds annoyed, but I know he isn't. He loves it when I tease him. Maybe even as much as I love teasing him.

I hum thoughtfully. "I *might* be willing to part with the

information if you let me stock pineapple for the snack-bar pizzas."

"Nobody is going to order that."

"They totally will, and if they don't, *I* still love it. You know I work my best when I have access to an optimal snack selection." My smile widens, enjoying the familiar twist of the muscles below my belly button as our banter escalates. Dar plays the part of grumpy and exasperated, I act playful and coy, and he caves to my demands *every single time*. It's addictive.

Do I know what's happening between us? No.

Am I loving it anyway? Yup.

Even if there's a little voice in the back of my head that will not shut up about me being reckless.

Dar groans, a sure sign that he's accepted defeat. "We'll try it. Just *try*, Savvy. Maybe there are other heathens in the area."

As I turn back to the computer, my heart is fluttering like a bird trapped in a cage. It's a good thing I haven't been paying attention to this, because the blaring alarm is worth the prospect of him coming back in here to do this all over again. "In that case. It's 4-3-2-1."

Silence.

"You must be joking."

"What?"

"That's a terrible code."

"Only terrible? Not dreadful? Or abhorrent? Abominable, perhaps? Good god, man, I thought you were a writer!"

Dar sighs heavily, already opening another window to change it. "Is all of the above an option?"

"It's not that bad when you think about it. A *truly* terrible code would have been 1-2-3-4. That's what everyone tries first. Once they do, and it doesn't work, they'll assume I'm savvy enough to come up with a proper code."

I feel him shaking his head, but when he answers, there's

a smile in his voice. "You're plenty *savvy*, Savvy. Though, if you used half the brain power necessary to get through that chain of logic, you'd have been able to pick and remember an actual secure code."

Humming, I settle back against him, watching as he clicks around. "Okay. New code?" Dar asks at last, his fingers poised over the keyboard.

It's hard to focus on anything this close to him, but I give it a shot. "1-1- 0-7."

He doesn't move to type it in, though, and my stomach begins that slow plummeting that always seems to follow an embarrassing moment. Finally, when I'm about to go limp and slip right between his arms and onto the floor like a wet noodle, he speaks. "That's my birthday."

"Is it?"

When I said it, I thought it would be... I don't know. Flirty, maybe? Cute? Now, it just feels like too much. After all, who remembers a family friend's birthday after nine years of complete estrangement? A loser who never quite managed to get over him, that's who.

Dar is silent as he inputs the numbers and closes out the window.

I glance at the time on the corner of the screen. "I think I'll take off for the night." It's only seven, and we've been here until nine the last couple of evenings. My car is back from the shop (though still making an ominous grinding noise that I'm ignoring because I can't afford to fix it), so he didn't have to drive me, and I'm grateful for the ability to make a clean escape.

Space. That's what I need. Dar and I have been holed up here together for weeks, working away in our little sexually frustrated—at least on my side—bubble. Admittedly, things have changed since our talk, but I can't let myself get carried away and start hoping for things that won't happen.

He said he was doing better, and I've seen evidence of that

with my own eyes, but that doesn't mean he wants me. Maybe what I see as playful, flirty banter, Dar sees as being friendly, or worse, *fatherly*. I've made that mistake before, and it was disastrous.

So, yeah, I need a few hours alone to get my head on straight. I'm going to go out wearing something scandalous, get hit on by a man I won't go home with, and remind myself that Darwin Wilder isn't my only option.

Then again, I couldn't get over him in nine years, so one night isn't likely to do the trick. This is my life now. I may as well lean into it and accept an existence riddled by hopeless longing. Besides, tomorrow is going to be a long day. Raven, her moms, and boyfriend, Jonah, are coming to help us clean the arena.

It's massive in there, taking up more space than the rest of Galactic Guild combined, and it's the only part of the business where Dad made regular updates and improvements. When you go in, especially with the flashing lights, fake smoke, and pulsing beat of the music in your ears, it's impossible not to get caught up in the fantasy of it all.

Unfortunately, every inch of the room is covered in dust, dirt, or trash thanks to Dad's dubious manager. Dar hasn't been doing a lot of cleaning, preferring to focus on the technology or repair side of things, and it would have taken me weeks to get the arena cleaned out if I didn't have help from Raven's family and our three new employees, who talk more than they work.

The hottest arms in the world disappear from either side of me as Dar straightens up. "Big plans?" he asks, and I can feel the weight of his eyes on me as I gather my things. I'm not sure if it's my imagination, but does he sound a little *too* casual?

I'm so unsettled tonight, restless even. Aside from the occasional touching and a bit of harmless banter, I've been Miss Responsibility for the last few weeks—working my ass off and fixing things instead of breaking them, all while guarding my heart from the unintentional charms of this man.

What is wrong with me? Nobody who has ever spent two minutes with Darwin Wilder could mistake him for charming, but I love—*nope*. Hard nope. I'm not even going to *think* about a sentence that has "Darwin Wilder" and "love" in it. Already, I've been getting too close to him, and if I'm not careful, I could end up falling right back into the place I was when I kissed a man who didn't want me. My pieced-together heart wouldn't survive a second fall.

Realizing I still haven't answered the question, I steel myself and turn. If there really is nothing here, my plans won't bother him. "I thought I'd go out, actually. Get a drink."

This time, I know I'm not imagining it when something darkens in Dar's expression. "Do you do that often?"

I shrug. "Nope. You know me, I'm more of a curl up at home with a good book kind of girl."

He folds his arms over his chest—his inconveniently hot arms over his inconveniently hot chest—lips turning down into his signature frown. "Why the sudden change of pace?"

My chin lifts, and I force myself not to turn away. "Maybe I want to meet someone. I enjoy sex. Haven't had it in a while."

Whoops, that was a little further than I wanted to take this. Sex is definitely not something you discuss with your dead dad's best friend, whom you are desperately trying not to fall for (again). I can't bring myself to regret it, though, because I *need* this reminder. Maybe we both do.

Dar doesn't just look bothered… He looks furious. "There are better solutions than finding a stranger to satisfy you. I know there's a shop just down the road that sells… equipment to assist with that."

It's saying a lot that even the scathing, cynical tone he's

using can raise the temperature in this office about twenty degrees. *Satisfy me?*

I swallow. "I'm not a pilgrim. I own a vibrator."

Dar takes a step forward, narrowing the distance between us to only a few feet, dark eyes boring into mine. "Use it, then." His voice is low and authoritative, inviting no discussion into the matter.

This conversation is getting out of hand so fast. I should leave it, laugh the whole thing off as a joke and live to fight another day.

I should—I would—except my heart is beating twice as fast as it should, and tension is crackling in the air between us. *I can't leave it.* Why should I when he's trying to give orders about what I should or shouldn't do with my vagina?

We're not in a relationship. How I choose to satisfy myself is none of his business.

"Would joining a dating app be better?" I ask, endeavoring to keep my voice sweet and bright, as if I'm oblivious to whatever the hell is going on and this is a totally normal discussion to be having with a man who once viewed me as his niece.

Dar obviously knows me well enough not to be fooled, or he's too pissed off not to bite. "No. It wouldn't," he snarls, and there's somehow only a foot between us now. I have to tilt my head back to maintain eye contact. Did I move closer? Did he? "Do you think they know what you need?"

My mouth falls open. "Do *you*?"

Silence.

All I can hear is our breathing, which is too ragged for two people just standing in an office. I've offered him an opening, a challenge, and he isn't taking it. The longer he goes without answering, the further my heart drops and the more certain I become.

He wants me.

He can't stand the idea of anyone else having me.

And it doesn't matter. If Dar doesn't feel the way I did about him nine years ago, badly enough to *risk it*, he may as well not feel anything at all.

Is that so much to ask for? To be *wanted*? For years, I was passed back and forth between my parents like a used tissue. They had their own lives, new relationships, new priorities, and I was just a consequence of their foolish teenage mistake. Then there was Dar, and after him, a string of relationships where I always seemed to care more than the other person in it.

It seems so clear now as I stand here staring at this man, who makes me feel seen, respected, and supported. This man who I realize—with a sensation akin to a kick to the chest— feels like coming home.

Feelings aren't enough. At some point, you have to act.

I want to be wanted.

I want to be fought for.

And now, *I want to get the hell out of here.*

Without bothering with goodbyes, I swipe my purse from the top of the desk and slip past the towering, mute statue who watches me go with a tortured expression.

My breaths tear painfully from my lungs as I stride down the hall toward the lobby, shoving open the employees-only door so hard that Luke, King, and Marley—who are chiseling calcified chewing gum off the bottom of the snack bar tables —stare.

"Good job today, guys!" I pause, forcing a bright smile for their benefit. "We got a lot done. I'm taking off, but Darwin will drive you home so you don't need to wait for the bus."

I've just made it to the front door when a voice calls out behind me, "Savvy!"

Shit.

Ignoring him, I shoulder it open and plunge into the parking lot toward my car.

"Savvy!"

Again, I pretend Dar isn't calling after me as I shove my hand into my bag, fumbling around for my keys and—*of freaking course*. I gave them to Marley hours ago when I sent her to get some stuff from my trunk.

Throat tight, I turn to face Dar as he jogs toward me. "I don't want to talk right now," I snarl when he stops four feet away, cold despite the unseasonably hot temperatures we've had all week.

Grave faced, he reaches into his pocket to produce my keys.

Oh god. As if this moment couldn't get any more humiliating. He wasn't even coming out here to talk to me.

"Thanks." I snatch them from his hand. "Don't worry, I'll *satisfy myself* with the vibrator tonight."

"I'm sorry. It wasn't… I don't know what I was thinking," he croaks, and I let out a hard laugh.

"Yeah, I'm sure. Don't worry about it."

"I *want* to worry about it." He steps toward me, then freezes, as if his body was acting without permission from his brain.

There's a big, hollow hole where my heart used to be, and finally, I shake my head. "You can't have it both ways, Dar."

He stares. Crickets chirp in the long grass across the street, kids laugh as they walk out of their karate class, the Earth spins on its axis, and still, Darwin Wilder just looks at me.

"I'll see you tomorrow," I promise as I turn toward my car, and the bitterness has drained from my voice.

After all, no one is to blame here but me.

CHAPTER 12
DARWIN

'VE PULLED my car into Stone's driveway more in the last week than I did in the entire time my friend lived here. He was more than happy to come to me, enjoying the luxury of free beer and playing our current video game obsession on a massive TV (that he convinced me to buy). Even if I *had* come here, however, I'm positive it wouldn't have felt like this.

I doubt the buzz of anticipation would have me glancing at my watch every thirty seconds, ready to leave far too early. There's no way I would drive with my heart lodged in my throat, fiddling with the AC or radio in an attempt to dispel some of this nervous energy.

None of this restlessness is from being out in public or knowing I'm about to encounter any number of viral plague–ridden strangers. It's all Savvy.

She texted me late last night, reporting more car trouble, and requested a ride to the hardware store before the cleaning campaign begins at Galactic Guild. I'd responded with all the unhinged enthusiasm of a thirteen-year-old boy whose crush asked for help with her history report. It was embarrassing.

Though, not as embarrassing as the following five

minutes, which I spent staring at my phone, waiting for her response of "ok".

I'm losing my shit.

It's not even eight in the morning, but my little tornado is still sitting on the steps, dressed and ready to go as planned. The moment she stands up, I know I'm in for a long day.

Summer is in full swing. It's hot out, and I could hardly expect her to cover up, but that doesn't make the sight of her walking to the car in high- waisted shorts and a crop top any less *affecting*. A sliver of creamy skin is visible between the garments, just wide enough for me to glimpse a dash of dark ink across her ribcage.

That fucking tattoo.

"Shit." I shift in my seat, willing my cock to stand down as Savvy opens the door and drops into the passenger seat. Her arms are full of her purse, clipboard, and a tumbler of iced coffee, which sloshes dangerously close to the top as she leans over to find her seatbelt. "Good morning."

"Morning," she mutters distractedly, digging through her purse. "Crap, I think I forgot my phone." Wordlessly, I reach over and pluck it out of the side pocket, and Savvy's cheeks flush pink as she takes it from me. "Thanks."

"No problem." I back out onto the street, hating the strain between us.

The last week together has felt like a dream. Never in my life has being with another person, even Stone, felt *easy*. The tension that once undercut every moment we spent together is gone, and what's left behind... Well, there is still tension, but of a very different variety. Every day, I feel myself edging closer to the point of no return, and with every innocent touch, my hope and confidence grows.

Maybe I can do this. Maybe I can have her.

Nine years ago, this woman followed her heart, even if it led her to ruin at my hands. I wasn't ready for her then, and she would have been miserable with me. She was too young, and I was too broken. It wasn't right, but that doesn't make her any less remarkable for trying.

If I want her, and it's impossible now to pretend I don't, it's my turn to be brave.

What she said last night, about me not being able to have it both ways, is true. It's time to make a choice—*the* choice—and it's terrifying.

Things have been good lately, but I know better than to believe my disorder is gone for good. I've let my guard down before, and if it weren't for Savvy coming back into my life when she did, things could have gotten a lot worse. It wouldn't be fair to put monitoring my mental health on her, though. If we got married…

I stop the thought in its tracks.

Married?

The woman in question hasn't said a word since we pulled out of her driveway, yet I'm imagining her walking toward me in a white dress with flowers in her hair.

I glance at her when we stop at a light, drumming my fingers on the steering wheel. Savvy is staring out the window, but her eyes are glazed, like she's not seeing any of it. Fuck, I can't stand this. "Savvy?"

She blinks and looks over at me, offering a tight smile. "Sorry."

The light turns green, and I drag my gaze back to the road. This woman has me in knots. How the hell do people get anything done when they have so many *feelings*? I've been so consumed by analyzing our every interaction that other worries have completely fallen off the radar.

I'm still trying to come up with something to say to ease the tension between us when we pull into the hardware store parking lot, which is crowded despite the early hour.

"You can stay in the car," Savvy offers as I park near the back of the lot, already slinging the strap of her bag over her shoulders. "It's just a few things."

"No. I'll come."

She pauses, looking over the center console at me, biting her lip. "It's always a madhouse in there, Dar."

"I'm fine." Probably. Hopefully. The ugly truth is that I haven't set foot in a large store like this one in years, and the prospect isn't inviting. This feels important, though, another test, another self-imposed boundary to be pushed, and I'm determined to get through it.

This newfound determination is likely related to my unwillingness to let Savvy out of my sight while she's dressed in that fucking outfit.

Neither of us say a word as we walk side by side across the parking lot and through the automatic doors. The place is packed with families and couples buying what they need to complete weekend projects, and just getting down the main aisle is a struggle. Displays of everything from power tools to cleaning supplies are boxing us in, and we're forced to stop whenever people in front of us do.

It's suffocating, and the farther we venture into the store, the more my chest tightens and my skin crawls.

"Do we have a list?" I ask, and there's no disguising the strain in my voice.

Savvy looks back at me, her caramel-colored eyes filled with worry. "You can wait in the car. If you want," she offers calmly. Apparently, whatever damage I inflicted last night isn't so grave that she isn't willing to set it aside to make sure I'm alright.

The battered organ in my chest pangs with affection for my pink-haired tornado.

"No," I insist, looking past her to watch two kids attempting to scale a pyramid of paper towels. "I'm fine. What do we need?"

Thankfully, she doesn't question me, instead lowering her eyes to her phone to check the list. "Looks like it's cleaning stuff. I want to make sure there are enough dusters and such for everyone. Oh! Also, we should grab a new light fixture for the men's bathroom while we're here. You know, that one above the sink that someone drew a dick on? I've scrubbed it like four times, but you can still see the hairy balls."

I snort, feeling a bit of the tension in my shoulders ease. "Are you sure? The dick light adds a lot of character."

Her lips twitch. "I'm not sure it fits the family-friendly vibe we're going for."

We turn down an aisle lined with hundreds of illuminated chandeliers and sconces. I trail after Savvy, clutching the handle of the cart like a lifeline. This section is thankfully quieter, and the harsh overhead lighting has been dimmed so shoppers can see the fixtures.

It's difficult to find anything good in this overcrowded testament to capitalism, but something deep inside my chest stirs to life as Savvy moves ahead of me. Her face is tilted back to examine the lights, which are casting a warm glow over her features.

And, out of nowhere, it hits me.

I haven't bothered with museums, or traveled, or encountered many exquisite things beyond the limits of my imagination. It's illogical, yet as I stand stock still watching Savvy Laurence gazing up at a display of bathroom sconces, *I know* she's the most beautiful woman in the world.

For my entire life, getting close to someone, physically or emotionally, was repulsive to me. People are messy in more ways than one, and Savvy… Savvy is the messiest. It makes no sense. Feeling this way about *anyone* else would be better, but I can't.

And now, I know I don't want to.

I hadn't realized it, but a timer started the moment I opened my door to find her there. Every day—*every minute*—I spend with her makes it harder to convince myself that I can't do this, that I want to be alone. I'm done trying.

Savvy has been back in my life for less than a month, yet has forced me to challenge every limitation I've set for myself.

I might not have much experience with falling in love, but I know now that's what this is. There's nothing I wouldn't do to keep her. There's no walking away from this, not for me. This woman is going to own me until the day I die, and I wouldn't have it any other way.

No more pretending. She deserves better. Fuck it. It's time.

"Dar?" Savvy turns, searching for me. I step out from behind the cart and move to her side in a trance, still rocked by the force of my realization. "What do you think?" She points above her head, but I can't bring myself to look away from her.

What do I think?

I think of reaching out and smoothing the little wrinkle between her eyebrows with my thumb.

I think of pulling her close and brushing aside pink hair so I can bury my face in her neck.

I think of backing her into the wall of boxes before us and kissing her senseless.

"Looks good," I manage.

Savvy nods, already looking for the correct box. "Shit," she mumbles, spotting it on the very top shelf and standing on her toes to reach.

I draw forward, my heart hammering against my rib cage. "Let me."

My hand settles on her waist, touching warm, bare skin as I reach over our heads to pull down the one she wants. My chest brushes her back. We're so close I can feel the warmth of her body through our clothing. I can hear her breath hitch.

If she were to shift back even an inch, there would be no hiding the effect she has on me.

"This one?" I ask, placing the box in her waiting hands.

Savvy nods, trembling so slightly I could have imagined it, but I didn't. Neither of us move.

"Is this okay?" My voice is so rough, so strained, that I barely recognize it.

We're in a public place. There are people on either end of the aisle, but we might as well be a thousand miles away from them. Nothing matters but this, and when Savvy nods, letting out a shaky breath, I could roar with triumph.

This is happening.

My hands tighten on her waist, pulling her more securely into me as I bow forward, brushing my lips over her pulse point. My cock is rock hard and settled perfectly against the curve of her ass. Savvy gasps, so quietly that even if someone were standing right behind us, they couldn't hear.

I'm doing this. *I'm* touching Savvy. It's my hands gripping her waist, my dick pressed against her ass, and my lips on her neck. This isn't accidental, or instinctive, or a goddamn handshake. This is me, a man, putting my hands on her, a woman I want with everything I am.

My head spins as I breathe in the fresh, sweet scent of her. Unable to resist, I brush my lips down, pressing a kiss to the soft skin where her neck and shoulder meet. The quiet whimper she makes is, without a doubt, the sexiest thing I've ever heard.

A cart passes noisily behind us, and I bet we look like any of the other couples here to the person pushing it: affectionate, happy, in love. Enjoying a quiet moment of intimacy while shopping.

There's no way for them to tell that an explosion is going off in my chest, or that my entire life is changing course in between the brightly painted shopping cart and a cardboard display of energy-efficient light bulbs.

I swallow, shoving away the last shadow of fear.

"You're all I've been able to think about for weeks," I tell her. At this angle, I can see the faint outline of her nipples, pebbled beneath that fucking top.

Maybe it's a good thing that we're in public and I don't

have unfettered access to her body. If I didn't... *fuck*. I don't want to think about what I'd do if I had her alone.

Savvy trembles, and the box she's grasping drops a few inches.

"I've never wanted anyone like this. Only you. Last night, the thought of you with someone else"—my hold on her waist tightens—"wrecked me, baby. If you don't feel the same, tell me to leave you alone. Tell me now, because the things I want to do to you aren't decent, and once we start..." Once we start, *I won't be able to stop.*

She's silent for so long that I worry, starting to feel the sharp edge of horror that she really will tell me no. I'd respect it, of course I would, but I'm not sure I'd ever recover from this—*from her*.

But then, "What kind of things?"

It's a miracle my knees don't give out.

Behind us, another cart rattles by, its driver giving a disapproving *tsk* at our public display of affection.

I clear my throat. "Later."

Savvy nods jerkily, and she's gripping the light box so tightly, the cardboard dents beneath her fingers. "Later," she confirms.

To Do: ⭐

~~Find a realtor for CC~~

~~Meeting with accountant~~
~~Find an accountant~~

Exact revenge on Caleb

Clean literally everything

Fix literally everything

~~Talk to HIM~~

~~New Vacuum~~

~~Rip up stained carpet in lobby + snack bar~~

~~Replace those long lightbulbs in the ceiling~~

~~Find out which games in arcade don't~~ work

~~Fix roof leak~~

~~Reconnect security system (at some point)~~

Find a therapist

~~Figure out why my car is making that clanky noise~~

New bathroom light fixture

~~Research competitor pricing~~

Complete the Google Ads course

Locate source of weird smell in back hallway

Buy tampons!!!!!!!!

Finish new website

Create social media graphics for Laser Speed Dating

Start ads on b-day parties

CHAPTER 13
SAVVY

DAR GETS a call from his agent almost the moment we get back in the car.

He stares at the caller ID with his jaw clenched, and finally jabs the accept button, wincing at me apologetically. A woman's voice fills the car, talking about some contract negotiation and throwing around lots of legal terms. She sounds mad.

I zone out. There are better things to think about, like the memory of Dar's hard cock pressed against my ass in the lighting aisle of the local hardware store or the words he murmured in my ear that made my heart race and my panties wet.

Only yesterday my life was an angsty Victorian drama, and now I've somehow stumbled into fifty shades of *holy crap*. It's disorienting and borderline terrifying, the effect he had on me. I'm hardly a virgin. I've had sex—and plenty of it—with people I *thought* I was attracted to.

However, none of them had the power to reduce me to a desperate, needy mess with only a few words. A desperate, needy mess who is about five seconds away from hitting end on a very important-sounding phone call and crawling over the center console to beg my father's best friend to let me ride his cock.

Wetness coats my panties at the thought, and I cross my legs, trying to relieve some of the ache. It doesn't work.

How could things have changed this fast? Only yesterday I was determined to put some space between us and save myself the inevitable heartache. Now… God, I don't know what to think.

We stop at the last light before the turnoff to Galactic Guild, and I suck in a sharp breath when a big, warm hand reaches and curls over my bare thigh. My head whips around. Dar is still speaking to his agent in a low, authoritative rush, but he's looking at me.

Heat tightens low in my belly even as the rest of my muscles melt back into the seat.

I need to be alone with him. Now. We need to talk, and… well, talk first. Talking is good. Sensible. There's a lot going on here, things that should be discussed before I bend over the nearest flat surface and let Darwin Wilder fuck me with every inch of—what felt like—his very considerable length.

He would too. It's like a switch has flipped inside the quietly intense, stern Dar, and the way he's looking at me… *Holy crap*, I'm going to start humping my own panties if I don't get a grip.

What he said in the hardware store… Just the thought of being the only woman Dar has ever wanted renews my desire to crawl onto his lap and commence begging.

If he were anyone else, I wouldn't stop to ask questions, but I can't just go for it. The two of us have history, and not all of it's good. Then, to top it all off, there's the added complication of his disorder and what happened the last time I kissed this man.

Just the memory of his disgusted, horrified face is enough to puncture the lusty bubble I've been floating in, allowing fear in.

Unfortunately, the fucking—*talking*—will have to wait. There's only one car in the parking lot of Galactic Guild, and four people are getting out: Raven, her moms, Penny and Julia, and her boyfriend, Jonah. Next to the door, King, Luke, and Marley are already waiting, eyeing us curiously.

God.

"We'll continue this tomorrow. Nothing will happen over the weekend, anyway," Dar says to his agent, his grip on my thigh tightening for just a second before he releases it and ends the call.

I swallow, waving at my favorite people while trying to look like my entire world *hasn't* just shifted on its axis.

"We should talk when they leave," he tells me quietly, busying himself with turning off the car.

"Later," I agree, already moving to open the door, but a big hand catches my wrist. I turn back to meet Dar's blazing stare.

"Just to be clear." His thumb strokes the delicate, translucent skin of my wrist, and goosebumps erupt all over my body. "I have feelings for you, I'm attracted to you, and I won't pretend otherwise. Not anymore."

My mouth pops open, but all I can manage is a splutter of shock before Dar releases his hold on me and turns to open his door.

As I watch him step outside and move toward the building, heart thundering in my chest, I meet the withering stare of my best friend.

And she's pissed.

———

"Darling, your aura is so faded." Raven's mother Penny sighs, smoothing my hair out of my face, her brow creased in worry. "Have you been practicing your self-care? Going to yoga?"

She's an acupuncturist, and the most maternal person I've ever met. Her wife, Julia, is a sociology professor at the local liberal arts college, and they still live in the same cozy bungalow where Raven and her brother grew up. There are paintings from local artists covering every inch of the walls, and the rooms smell like incense and the lavender Penny grows in her garden.

Unlike my parents, who divorced before I could speak in complete sentences, Penny and Julia Cho-Hopkins seem to genuinely like each other, and so do their adult kids. The entire family goes on vacations together and has dinner every Sunday night. When someone graduates or gets a promotion, they throw a party to celebrate. When Raven's brother, Kai, broke both wrists snowboarding, they all rushed to the hospital. They're here now, giving up their entire day to clean a laser tag arena for their daughter's childhood best friend.

I love them.

"Trying to," I assure her, smiling halfheartedly.

Penny is unconvinced. "You need to nurture yourself, Savvy. Physically, emotionally, sexually—"

Behind us, there's a loud choking noise, and I turn to see Dar with a bottle of water held loosely in his hand, a bright-red face, and a dark stain spreading down the front of his shirt.

I raise my eyebrows at him, trying not to laugh at his deer-in-headlights look.

"Sorry." He shakes his head. Ignoring all the eyes on him, he marches toward the door while muttering about getting a fresh shirt from his car.

"What," demands Julia the moment he's gone, "is going on *there*?"

It's my turn to choke, and, judging by the heat that's rushing to my face, I'm pretty sure my face is just as red as his was. "What do you mean?" I squeak.

"Leave her alone, mom," says Raven firmly, even as she glowers at me behind her mother's back.

"There's a vibe," Jonah adds unhelpfully. Raven elbows him in the ribs.

Are we that obvious? They couldn't have seen him touching me.

"So, I think we have everything we need!" I chirp, determinately cheerful as I pull away from Penny to examine the pile of cleaning stuff we set up on a folding table. "This is really amazing of you guys to help with all this. Thank you again. We'll order pizza in a few hours for lunch."

"Of course, sweetheart." Julia kisses my cheek as she passes, heading for the arena with a trash bag and rubber gloves in hand. Her wife follows, and suddenly, I'm alone with my best friend and her boyfriend.

The last few weeks have been hectic. We've texted a bit, but I haven't told her anything about what's been happening with Dar. How could I when even I don't understand it?

Those excuses aren't likely to hold up with Raven, though.

"Okay, what the hell?" she demands, craning her neck to make sure Dar isn't returning. "You guys looked ready to make out in the car when you pulled up. What is going on?"

"I have no idea," I admit, shaking my head. "There's... something. We haven't talked about it."

Raven gapes at me. "Doesn't he *not do* people? Or dirt? I thought when you said he was helping with all this, you meant financially. Not, like, doing stuff!" She gestures around at the lobby, which looks so much better than it did when she was last here. "You were in love with the guy for years, then broken up over what happened for even longer. Are you actually—" She stops mid sentence as Dar slips back inside, wearing a fresh T-shirt and looking more composed than when he left.

"Thank you again for your help today," he tells Raven and Jonah graciously, moving to stand beside me.

Raven glowers at him. "Of course. *We* care about Savvy."

If her veiled hostility phases Dar, he doesn't show it. On the contrary, instead of walking away or pretending nothing is amiss, he wraps an arm around my waist, tucking me close to his side.

My heart stalls. When he said that in the car, I didn't think… but there's no room for misinterpretation here.

Should I be happy? Scared? Anxious? Everything is happening so fast.

Since when has fast bothered me? I love fast.

If looks could kill, Raven would have reduced Dar to dust. "She was messed up for *years* because of those things you said," she spits, planting her hands on her hips. "What's changed? Are you having a mid-life crisis and want a hot twenty-seven-year-old on your arm? Or is it just that Stone is out of the way, and now you can fuck his daughter without feeling guilty?"

"Raven!" I gasp, horror clogging my throat. "Stop—"

"It's okay, Savvy," says Dar, and his voice is calm, unaffected by the accusations she just hurled at him. His hold on me tightens. "It's neither, actually. I sought treatment for my obsessive-compulsive disorder. Unfortunately, I was having something of a severe episode at the time Savvy came back into my life, and she pulled me out of it. More than that, she's made me realize how much I've been limiting myself. She's also the most beautiful, creative, compassionate woman I've ever known. So, yes. I have feelings for her. Of course I do."

I can't breathe, I doubt I could even move. All I can do is stand here, listening, as these words change me from the inside out.

Dar continues without pause, sounding so matter-of-fact, it's like he's had these words prepared for a long time. "She's been your best friend for most of your life if I'm not mistaken, so surely you've realized the kind of person she is. Well, now I know too. Every minute we spend together, I'm more in awe of her. I have no doubt you'll see this as selfish, but if she wants me, I'd be a fool not to fight for the chance to make her happy."

Ringing silence follows this speech.

Raven stares, lips pursed and fists balled at her sides. Beside her, Jonah shifts awkwardly, scratching his head. I look between them, then up at Dar's nonchalant expression, as though he did nothing more remarkable than give her directions to the post office.

And then I burst into tears.

There's no stopping it, no way to hold it back. This is so much more than I even thought to hope for. Dar isn't feigning indifference, or easing into this, or playing the game of *who-cares-less emotional chicken* that all my other relationships have begun with. He's in this every bit as much as I am.

Darwin Wilder is just as gone for me as I am for him. Maybe even more.

"Let's give them a minute, Rave," I hear Jonah say, but I don't see them leave because my hands are pressed over my face. As if in covering my tears, I could play this off as anything other than some kind of emotional break. They must be gone, because a second later, Dar pulls me into his warm, coffee-smelling chest.

"I'm sorry," he murmurs, stroking my hair. "I'm so sorry, Savvy. That was a lot—" But I'm shaking my head, and he stops speaking, waiting for me to get it together enough to communicate.

I can't do it, though. I'm so totally unprepared for all this. How long have I guarded my heart from this man, trying to convince myself that I'm not feeling what I am? Well, now it's all hitting me at once, and there's no stopping it.

Oh, fuck. I love him, don't I?

I do. I totally do.

Did I ever stop?

Dar doesn't seem to mind. He holds me close, murmuring

quiet, reassuring words in my ear as one hand strokes up and down my spine.

I have enough self-awareness and shitty life experiences under my belt to know I'm not a cute crier. My face gets blotchy and red, my eyes get swollen, and my nose runs. So, it's saying a lot that Dar is still looking down at me with an expression of nothing but unguarded devotion when my tears stop and I'm able to look up at him.

"God, I'm sorry. I feel like I'm always crying on you." I let out a watery laugh, my bottom lip trembling. "Please don't run away screaming now that you've seen how crazy I am."

Dar laughs quietly, smoothing his thumbs over my cheeks to wipe away the last of my tears. "You're much less crazy than I am. I've caused you too much pain for one lifetime, little tornado. What I said in the car, and to Raven… I meant it."

I lift my hand, pressing it flat against the place above his heart. "I know you did."

His pulse stutters under my touch, and his handsome face is creased with worry. "Savvy. I can't promise this will be smooth sailing. My disorder—"

"I understand," I assure him, calm despite my wildly beating heart. *Is this really happening?* "We'll take it slow. Figure it out together."

No one has ever looked at me the way he is right now. "I'm too old for you. Way too old."

Does he think that's going to phase me? My lips curl. "I think it's pretty clear I'm into it."

His hands are still cradling my face, and my smile vanishes as quickly as it came when the pad of his thumb drags over my bottom lip. "You're too beautiful for me."

"Are you fishing for compliments, Mr. Wilder?" Giving him every chance to pull away, I part my lips and lean forward to take the tip of his thumb in my mouth, biting down gently.

Dar's pupils dilate, and the look on his face is one of pure, visceral hunger. "Make no mistake, Miss Laurence. I might be playing the gentleman now, but if you let me between those thighs, I won't tolerate teasing."

Oh god. Every fantasy I've ever had of this man is beginning to look like a terrible underestimation. Hell yeah. Sign me up.

Releasing my teeth's hold on his thumb, I step away, grinning as I back toward the cleaning supplies. "Fair warning, I'm probably going to tease anyway."

He smiles back at me, a huge, unrepentant smile that sends an eruption of butterflies through me. "Good."

CHAPTER 14
DARWIN

"WELL, I think it's safe to call this a breakthrough, Darwin."

I've been seeing Doctor Lucas for over five years now, and I've never seen him look so pleased. It's unsettling. "I don't know if I'd go that far," I say, leaning back in my office chair.

Lucas laughs. "Why the hell not? A month ago, you were in a very different place. A *bad* place, and I believe you'll agree. When I saw you'd finally kept an appointment, I expected the worst. But you're telling me you've been leaving the house regularly, working in a non-sterile environment, went to a large store, and are in an intimate relationship. Anything else I should know about?"

There is, and I'm not sure why I'm embarrassed to admit it. I scratch my beard, staring at the wall beyond my computer screen. "I've been writing. Quite a lot. It's not anything yet, but it might be."

The man looks, if possible, even happier. "Oh, is that all? Do me a favor and lift your hands for me to see."

Reluctantly, I do as he asks. They look normal, or at least close. There are darkened patches in the places where my skin once cracked. They're not scars, but are still an obvious reminder of where I was not so long ago.

Doctor Lucas grins. "Goddamn, Wilder. I'm impressed. Tell me more about this woman."

Ah. This is the part of the conversation I wasn't looking forward to. "Her name is Savvy." My therapist arches an eyebrow, and I continue, "She's... Stone's daughter. I offered to help her with Galactic Guild, and we grew close."

That has his attention. "Can I ask how old she is?"

I refuse to hide my feelings for Savvy, but that doesn't make the topic of our age difference any less awkward to broach. "She's twenty-seven."

To my surprise, Lucas chuckles and shakes his head. "Not as bad as I feared. We'll get back to that. So, she's aware of your history?"

"She is."

He makes a note on the pad in front of him. "And, have you been physically intimate?"

It's a testament to how truly gone for this woman I am that my therapist saying the words "physically intimate" in reference to her makes my cock twitch.

"No," I admit, grateful there's a desk covering my lap. "We're taking it slow."

Slow is good. It's the sensible thing to do, given my mental health and our history. Plus, Savvy *deserves* romance for all that I've put her through. I can't go from pretending our relationship is platonic to dry humping her against the snack bar in the space of a few days.

Even if it's all I've been able to think about.

Lucas hums, still scribbling. "Is that something you're worried about, considering your history of aversion to physical contact?"

I hesitate. "Savvy... Understands. Better than most would. If there are issues, we'll figure it out."

"You're avoiding the question."

I drum my fingers on the surface of the desk, staring blankly at a stack of notes I made late last night as I search for the honest answer. *Yes.* Yes, I'm fucking worried about it. After all we've been through so far, we haven't even kissed, and the prospect is equally thrilling and terrifying. Memories of the last time her lips touched mine keep coming to mind, a sobering reminder of how badly this could go.

Wanting her isn't an issue. Even before we settled things yesterday, I've had to jerk off twice a day just to take the edge off, and it's always to thoughts of Savvy. Sometimes, if she's worn something truly agonizing that day, I'll press my face in a sweater she left in my car as I work myself, my hips lifting off the bed as her scent invades my senses.

I've thought of burying my face between her thighs, sucking away the sweet cream her pussy has made for me. I've wondered how it would feel to push my fingers inside her tight hole and watch myself pump them in and out, searching for the place that makes her shake.

So, yes. I'm worried.

Before I can think of a way to tell all this to Lucas, however, an alarm on his phone chimes. My therapist smiles wryly as he silences it. "Saved by the bell. Listen, Darwin, I'll just say this. For a long time, you had something of a codependent relationship with your OCD. As terrible as it was, it also enabled you to avoid stepping out of your comfort zone. From the sounds of it, you're out now. Enjoy yourself."

Lucas promises to have his receptionist call and set up my next appointment, and we end the call, leaving me alone in my silent house.

It's the middle of the day, and Savvy is working at her driving job for another few hours. I haven't seen her since yesterday evening, when her friend's family swept her off to have dinner with them after a day spent cleaning the arena. I declined their invitation, sensing Raven would stab me with a fork if I accepted the offer. Instead, I drove home to my big, dark, empty house.

Funny how so recently, this was the most comforting place in the world to me. Now, it's missing something. Someone. What would change about this room if Savvy lived here? What would it be like to open the bedroom closet and see my clothes hanging side by side with hers? To kiss her awake? To be the person she comes to when she has a fight with her mother or is struggling with work?

Fuck, I'm in this so deep. I'm never going to recover from this—from her—and, seemingly overnight, my priorities have shifted. The gaping hole in my chest that's been present since the release of my last book is closing up, and, as difficult as it is for me to admit it, so is my grief for Stone.

I'll always miss him and be grateful for his friendship, but there was so much left unsaid between us, so many resentments never voiced. I also can't forgive him for the position he left Savvy in, or for not at least setting aside his shame to prepare her for it.

She is my priority now.

Doctor Lucas was right. It was easier to face my OCD than it was to face myself, but I have now. It's so obvious in retrospect how restricted I was, how much I was allowing my disorder to control me when I was more than capable of controlling it. If I'm going to make her happy, I'll need to keep trying.

I have to do something. Something deliberate and planned that isn't falling all over myself to get closer to her.

We *are* close. Against all odds, things I never dared to hope for are *happening*, and I refuse to take them for granted. Now comes the real work: building a foundation we can grow on, because this *needs* to last. I don't want her to think she was something that just happened to me. Savvy deserves to feel chosen, adored, and special, and while I have no practical knowledge of how to do this, I'm determined to figure it out.

Pulling out my phone, I lean back, thumbs hovering over the screen as I try to decide how to go about this.

> The kids aren't working, so let's play hooky tonight. Galactic Guild can wait until tomorrow.

I slide my phone onto the desk, not expecting her to get back to me any time soon, and turn to my computer. There's an open document with ideas for my next project, but even as I attempt to work, all I do is rewrite the same sentence five times, aware of the silent phone sitting beside my hand.

When it buzzes a few minutes later and I nearly drop the device in my hurry to see her response, I'm very glad there's no one to witness it.

> Savvy: This is awfully irresponsible, Mr. Wilder. I support it. I'm kind of bummed I won't see you though…

> Savvy: Is that weird to say? I'm sorry if that was super awkward.

> Darwin: It is weird to say, because you won't miss me.

> Darwin: I was unclear before. Let's play hooky together. Come to my house when you're finished working?

> Savvy: Yes, please.

———

By the time the sun is setting and I know Savvy should be finished with work, I'm beginning to second-guess this plan.

Isn't the whole point of making a gesture like this to show her I've changed? Would it have been better to take her out somewhere? There are dozens of highly rated restaurants within ten minutes of us, but instead of taking her to one of them, I spent the better part of the day doing *this*? Truthfully, I've had more than enough self-imposed challenges for one week and wanted to be able to focus on her, not the panic clawing at my insides or resisting the urge to scrub my hands until the feeling stops. What if that was the wrong thing to do, though?

I scrub my hand over my face, surveying the carefully laid table and the flickering candles, and beyond that, the telescope I've set up on the back deck beside all the blankets and pillows I could find. It's supposed to be a clear night, and there have been meteor showers all summer. If we're lucky, maybe we can catch one.

That's romantic, isn't it?

As I arranged it all, I imagined myself showing Savvy how to adjust the settings, pointing out the planets visible from our hemisphere with my arms around her... Fuck, who *am* I?

I barely recognize the thoughts I'm having, can barely wrap my head around the fact that this is my life now. This might all be new to me, but it feels good. *Right.* Never in my adult life have I felt so free of my compulsions, as close to typical as someone like me can ever hope to be.

Tonight, I'm not a man trapped by his own mind. I'm Savvy's boyfriend. Hopefully. Maybe. If she'll have me.

My stomach twists, because *I don't know.* My actions thus far certainly seemed to express how I feel, haven't they? The things I said yesterday suggested as much, but I still haven't heard how she feels about this particular plot twist. Maybe it's all too much, too fast. I have no idea what I'm doing, and I've never resented my lack of romantic experience so much until now.

There's no time to reconsider this plan, though, or try to recall how I've gone from obsessive recluse to hopelessly besotted boyfriend (hopefully) in under a month. Headlights shine through the front windows, and my heart takes up residence in my throat as I cross to the front of the house

I linger behind the heavy wood door, wiping my sweaty palms on my jeans. The doorbell sounds a minute later, but I force myself to pause where I am and not lunge for the handle like the deranged lunatic I've clearly become.

When I do open it, though, I wish I hadn't resisted.

Savvy looks up at me from the front step, dressed in a little white sundress that makes her skin look gold in contrast, and she's smiling.

"Hi," I choke out, dazed by how unbelievably gorgeous she is. Her smile widens. "Hi."

I step aside, allowing her past me into the house. Only a few weeks ago, I opened this door and was nearly bowled over by my reaction to her. It seems like so much longer ago than it was; everything feels so different now.

I know now that this isn't just attraction. I've fallen for her and, as we walk side by side back into the kitchen, I realize how terrifying it is not to know if she's feeling this as deeply as I am.

Savvy stops as we enter the kitchen, and I hear her gasp. "Dar," she breathes, eyes shining in the dimmed lights. "You did all this? For me?"

My stomach sinks as I watch her take in the table, the telescope, and the food. There's no question about my intention for tonight to be a date. "Is it too much? I didn't want to—" My words falter, and I look away from her, staring at the table without seeing it. "I'm sorry if it's too much."

A soft, warm hand takes mine, squeezing, and I gather my courage to turn back to her.

Savvy doesn't look upset. "It's not too much." She shakes her head. "It's amazing, Dar. I don't know what to say. Nobody's done something like this for me before."

I feel a prickle of irritation toward her previous boyfriends for failing so spectacularly, but it doesn't take long to vanish. If they'd treated Savvy the way she deserves, we wouldn't be here now. Even if it's selfish, I can't bring myself to regret their negligence.

Emboldened, I reach out, tucking a lock of pink hair back behind her ear. "I've never done this for anyone, either."

Her answering smile is—quite literally—breathtaking. "But you did for me."

I'll do a lot more if I can make her mine. Everything. Anything. My gaze moves to her lips, watching the tip of her pink tongue dart out to wet them. "Yes," I tell her at last.

Neither of us move, and something seems to tighten in the space between us as the room floods with heat.

We're standing in almost the same spot we were nine years ago and, judging by the sudden flash of apprehension on Savvy's face, she realizes it too. As she goes to step away, though, my hand darts out to stop her.

I can't hear anything over the blood rushing in my ears.

Savvy gazes up at me from beneath her eyelashes, full lips parted.

Perfect. She's perfect.

It's as though the gravity in the foot between us is stronger, and resisting the pull is almost impossible. Something defiant rears inside me as I realize how fearful she looks, how worried she is that this moment will be a repeat of the last time we stood in this spot.

As I lean down to slant my mouth over Savvy's in a kiss, it's almost an out-of-body experience.

I see it from the outside as her mouth opens to mine, and hear the rough, hungry noise I make in response.

I see her hands fly to my chest as mine find her waist, squeezing harder than I should in my desperation.

I see the way we rock together, her body bowing to mine, as our kisses turn from sweet to frantic in seconds.

She's made me so hard it's painful, an urgent, throbbing

ache that I know instinctively can only be relieved by her. I need to fuck her, need to feel my little tornado from the inside, to pump and pump until we're so lost in each other that we'll never find our way apart.

Fuck, I didn't know it was possible to want anything this much.

My hands find her breasts, cupping and teasing them greedily through the soft material of her dress. She feels incredible, feminine and warm against my larger, harder body. I want to bury my face in her stomach and breathe her in, but before that, I need to make her come.

"Savvy, baby." I tilt my hips forward, showing her how hard she's made me and drawing a gasp from her swollen lips. "You feel so good."

"So do you. Oh god, *Dar*, don't stop," she pleads brokenly, pressing against me as my mouth reclaims hers.

Our kiss grows unrestrained and bruising. In my arms, my little tornado is writhing, moaning, and arching her back, trying to get closer to me. I know what she needs, know it with such confidence it's like I've stepped inside her skin.

Reaching down, I grip the back of her thighs and lift, never once moving my lips from hers. It's as if we choreographed this. There are no awkward pauses or fumbling hands, no clacking teeth or discomfort. No, our bodies have been waiting for this a lot longer than our heads would like us to believe. We're ready.

Savvy hisses in surprise when the bare skin of her thighs meets the cold marble countertop, but I don't pause.

Dragging the hem of her little white dress up over her head, my eyes roam hungrily over bare, golden skin. They don't get far.

My cock is going to tear through these fucking pants —*Jesus Christ.*

I groan, my entire body vibrating with the effort it takes not to lunge at her. "Oh fuck, baby. You pierced them?"

Savvy smiles coyly, her cheeks flushed and breathing ragged. "Do you like it?" Sitting forward, she wraps her hands around my wrists, guiding them up to cup her bare tits.

Holy fuck.

"You're perfect." It's not an exaggeration. The more I look, the more sure I become. Those piercings are hot as fuck, and when I manage to tear my eyes away from them, I'm rewarded with a full view of the tattoo that's been tormenting me for weeks.

It's like the artist sprinkled a section of the night sky over the skin of her rib cage. Black and deep-blue ink swirl together, with tiny pinpricks of space left in the ink, allowing her skin to shine through like the light of distant suns.

Emotion clogs my throat as I remember the telescope set up outside, but it's nothing compared to the rush of raw devotion that comes when I can read the text scrawled along the top of it.

It's good for the plot.

My eyes lift to her face as shocked recognition settles over me. She has my words tattooed on her body?

"I got it the week I turned eighteen," Savvy explains quietly, and there's uncertainty in her face now, as though I could be anything other than awed by her. The thought of her carrying this piece of me on her skin for all these years…

My fingers ghost over the tattoo, half expecting to feel some difference in the inked skin, but there's none. It's a part of her. *I'm* a part of her.

How many times is this woman going to rob me of the ability to speak?

It doesn't matter. Right now, we don't need to talk.

My fingers knot in the back of her hair, and Savvy's surprised gasp has barely left her lips before I've dragged her back into me to kiss her with everything I have.

The choreography has changed now. The frantic, dumb

lust that possessed me only moments ago has been replaced with a dark, primal need that goes so much deeper.

She was made for me, and now I'm going to fucking take her.

Savvy cries out, panting into my mouth as my hands return to her tits, drawing my thumbs back and forth over the tiny metal balls nestled on either side of the puckered flesh. "So naughty, baby," I grit out in between kisses.

Her body arches into my touch and—fuck—I've never been so hard. Never. I'm making her feel this way. *Me.* My hands are on her body. Her dress is laying in a crumpled heap on my floor, and I'm the one who put it there.

This stunning, fearless creature wants *me.* And I want to make her come. Repeatedly.

My hands drop to her hips, and we steal harsh, desperate kisses as Savvy lifts her ass, letting me pull down her panties. They've only just cleared her ankles before I've sealed our bodies together again. I can't stop touching her, and I don't want to. Never have I felt so utterly out of control, so outside my own head. I'm operating on instinct alone, and it's exhilarating.

Part of me wants to make this last, to draw out every second for as long as possible and remember every gasp or moan I draw from her body. As Savvy's naked legs wrap around me, though, her hands clutching my shirt, I know it's a lost cause.

"You need this so bad, don't you?" I ask, lowering my head to suck roughly on her neck, hard enough to leave a mark. The need to make this woman mine in every way is driving me out of my mind.

I feel, rather than see, her nodding in response. "Yes—*oh my god*—yes, Dar!" She's grinding against me, pressing those perky, hot-as-fuck tits against my chest. I tilt her back to take one in my mouth, sucking greedily and batting her piercing with my tongue.

I want more.

I want to worship this woman, to make her feel so good that she forgets every other man who's touched her. A savage growl breaks from my chest at the thought, and my hands find her bare ass, dragging her to the edge of the countertop.

Her pussy is pressed against my stomach, the heat of her searing even through my shirt.

"I'm going to make you come," I promise as I switch to her other breast, worshiping this side as fiercely as the first.

Savvy's hands tighten in my hair. "Please!"

"Look at you," I rasp, straightening up and gazing between us at her naked body. "I never stood a chance, did I? Holy fuck, you're going to look so good stretched around my cock, baby."

Goosebumps erupt over her body, and I know they're not from the cold.

She likes it when I call her that, likes it when I praise her beautiful body. "Can I touch you?" I keep my eyes on hers, searching for signs that this is going too fast as my fingers drag over the delicate skin of her inner thigh, edging closer to her pussy.

Savvy's eyelids flutter as she spreads her legs further, making room for me. "You can do anything you want."

Her words make me throb. There's a thousand things I want to do to her, an endless list of desires that begin and end with making my girl moan. I may not have done this before, but I'm going to figure it out. *I have to.*

As I move to touch her, though, something shifts inside me.

No. No. No.

Instead of moving to Savvy's pussy, my hand drops to the counter, curling into a fist as the familiar too-hot, crawling discomfort seeps through me. I swallow, forcing myself to breathe through my nose.

"Dar?"

I can't look at her, so I turn away, frustration and horror taking root inside me, warring with the lust that was so potent only seconds ago. "Just a second," I tell her, and my voice is strained. Part of me wants to turn around and take what's mine, while the other—the stronger, more familiar part —wants to end this. To walk straight to the sink and turn the water on as hot as it will go, to clean and clean until I rid myself of the horrible, clawing thoughts that have violated the best moment of my life.

Fuck—*God fucking damn it.* How will I ever look her in the eye again? How will I ever convince her I want her more than anything, when my actions say the opposite?

"Dar." Savvy's hands find my face, guiding me toward her again. Even through my panic, my heart wrenches at the softness in her expression. "Tell me what you're thinking."

I swallow, shaking my head as I try to break away from my spiraling thoughts, humiliation and guilt burning in my chest.

"Dar," she insists, leaning forward and pressing the sweetest kiss to my jaw. "Let me in. *Please.*" And there's no mistaking the strain in her voice. I realize with a jolt that it isn't my disorder stopping tonight in its tracks, it's my reluctance to open up to her.

My eyes squeeze shut. "I'm thinking there's something… something in your… it will burn me." I can't say it, I just can't. That my brain is trying to tell me that the slick, shiny wetness coating Savvy's beautiful pussy, physical proof of her attraction to me, is anything other than glorious… This is my worst nightmare come to life.

Except, Savvy seems to understand without me needing to say it. "Dar," she murmurs, holding my gaze. "Watch."

I watch.

My heart leaps into my throat as one slim hand slides teasingly down her bare body. By the time she dips two fingers between the lips of her pussy, coating them in her own arousal, I can't breathe.

"Watch," she whispers again, lifting those same fingers to her mouth.

Before I can even process what her intention is, she's wrapped her lips around her fingers, sucking away her own wetness.

My cock throbs, and I make a rough, wounded noise. "Baby—"

"See?" Savvy murmurs, and before I can recover from the gesture, she does it again. "I won't hurt you, Dar. I promise."

For a moment, all I can do is stare. I love her.

This woman, who's made friends with my inner monsters, who's shown me the world isn't something to hide from... I'm in love with her.

I'm so in love with her, I'll never recover. So in love, that if I dedicated the rest of my life to writing out my devotion to Savvy Laurence, I still wouldn't come close to capturing the intensity of my feelings for her in this moment.

My hands have relaxed, and, forcing myself to go slow, I reach for her again.

Savvy meets my kiss without hesitation, arching closer to me, and the cold metal of her piercings brushes my chest.

I can taste her arousal on her lips, and a guttural groan breaks free from my chest as our kiss turns from reverent to hungry in seconds. We're in the same position we were before I pulled away, and the lust kindling between us is just as potent. It's as though no time has passed, like we never stopped.

Savvy isn't put off by what just happened, she hasn't gone cold or become self-conscious. She understands me and sees all of me, even the parts I wish she didn't have to, and she wants me anyway.

It takes every ounce of control I possess to keep from dropping to my knees and telling her right now.

I love you.

I'm going to love you for the rest of my life.

"Savvy," I plead, my head falling back as my little tornado attacks my neck, kissing, licking, and biting like I did to her only minutes ago. "I want to eat your pussy, baby. Let me make you feel good—"

"Baby steps," she murmurs, even as her hand finds the hard ridge of my cock, stroking me through my pants and making me shake. "I have an idea."

CHAPTER 15
SAVVY

'M stark naked in the middle of Darwin Wilder's kitchen, my ass resting on his pristine marble countertops and my panties hanging off the dining chair behind him.

Dar's throat works as I push him back gently, allowing me room to slip off the counter and onto the cold wood floor. "I want to make you feel good," he whispers, voice hoarse and his big hands coming up to frame my neck. "Please don't treat me like I'm going to break."

My answering laugh is breathless and disbelieving. "I don't think you're going to break. You're the strongest person I know." My hands settle on his broad, hard chest, loving the way I can feel his heart thudding beneath my touch.

What just happened between us was the most imperfect, intimate moment of my life. When he drew back, his body tense and expression crumpled with frustration... I wanted to crumple too. My pride wanted me to scramble away, to take it as a second earth-shattering rejection, and never allow myself to be put in such a position again.

This wasn't the same as it was nine years ago, though. Dar wants me. This beautiful, intense, genius of a man wants me, and I want him.

He isn't playing games or pretending not to care.

He isn't pushing me aside, even though I'm positive it would be a lot easier.

He saw my tattoo, physical proof of the place he's always held in my life, and he didn't run screaming.

Nothing, not even his disorder, is going to take tonight from us.

Careful not to break eye contact, I press forward, guiding him back toward the kitchen table.

I barely blink as Dar sinks into a chair beside the beautiful dinner he made just for me—which we will absolutely get to later. I'm positive I've never felt so special, so wanted. His gaze is worshipful, and I draw closer, winding my fingers through his hair as he attacks my breasts all over again, igniting a need inside me that's so intense, it's almost painful.

Never have I been so in sync with another person. I'm not self-conscious, or wondering if he's ever going to call me after this, or worried if he approves of my personal grooming preference.

"I want to be everything you need." The words come out before I can think to hold them back, before socially awkward red flags start waving in my line of vision, reminding me to *slow down*.

Dar doesn't mind. A low, rough noise of shock leaves his lips as he looks up at me again, pupils blown wide from the intensity of the moment. "Baby, I want to be that for you."

Baby.

I never want him to stop calling me that. Just the sound of that word on his lips makes every muscle in my body go weak and my heart twist restlessly, undoubtedly knowing it's in for one hell of a ride.

I sink to my knees, and Dar's face registers surprise for all of half a second before something else takes its place, something dark and unrestrained. Gazing up at him from beneath my lashes, I lean forward and kiss the straining ridge of his erection.

Dark eyes flash. "I bet you like it dirty, huh?"

Holy crap. My inner walls contract, suddenly so empty. Nobody has ever talked this way to me before, and to know those words are coming from tightly wound Dar?

Well, not so tightly wound anymore, because I'm unraveling him. All that control has finally snapped, and I'm on the receiving end.

"I do." My voice is breathy, and I squirm at his feet, wetness spreading onto my inner thighs. How many times have I made myself come while imagining what it would be like for Darwin Wilder to lose himself in my body? Too many to count.

There's a low curse from the beautiful man above me. "When I fuck you for the first time, do you want it sweet and romantic or hard and rough?"

Yeah, pretty sure we both know what I'm going to say to that, but god, hearing him say that… My hands tighten on his hard thighs. "I want to feel you inside me even when you're not anymore."

He likes that. A lot. Chest heaving, two big hands fist in my hair, rough enough to make my scalp burn. "And what about now, baby?"

I feel my lips curl into a coy, teasing smile. "I want you to use my mouth."

A second of silence, then two. This is the point where I'd start worrying that I've said the wrong thing or ruined the vibe, but the look on Dar's face leaves no doubt that he's into this. *Very* into this.

His throat bobs, and when he speaks again, his voice has dropped to a strained authority. "Take my cock out, Savvy."

The way he says it, just a little impatient, makes heat shoot through my veins. I feel like I'm shaking with need, but my hands are steady as they move to the metallic button on

Dar's pants. It gives easily, and the muscles below my belly button pull tighter and tighter as I tug the zipper, which is obviously having some difficulty maintaining its structural integrity, what with the very large, very hard dick pressing against it.

The poor thing seems to be relieved to give up the fight and pulls down easily, letting me reach beneath the band of his briefs and wrap my hand around the thick base of Dar's cock.

Oh god. There's no way… Even as I think it, though, a thrill of excitement shoots through me, making my clit throb.

"Of course you're massive." I giggle as I draw his length into the light. A quick glance up confirms that while Dar might be above the majority of XY-chromosome havers on some matters, he isn't immune to some male smugness. His hips twitch as I begin to stroke him.

I want to ask if he likes it, but Dar clearly isn't interested in this becoming question-and-answer time. "Use your mouth." His voice is pure, commanding control, and, just like that, a hot weight settles in my pelvis. All questions about his sexual preferences are forgotten in the face of the filthy, perfect words being uttered by the man I've wanted for *so long*. "Suck me, baby."

Moaning, I drop my head forward and lick the head of his cock decadently, lapping away the pre-cum that's already gathered there. Saliva flows freely over my tongue as I wrap my lips around his shaft, taking what I can't fit in my hands.

We both need this. Me, to feel like an object of his desire after being convinced of the opposite for so long. Him, to take control of his own pleasure and to trust me when I tell him I want him.

And I *do* want him. More than anything.

There's nothing sexier in the whole world than Dar losing his cool because of how good I'm making him feel. He holds back at first, his low grunts and ragged breathing the only sign he's enjoying this at all. His face tells a different story, though.

The more he tries to restrain himself, the more determined I become to make sure he *can't*.

"That's so good, *holy fuck*, that mouth..." I bob faster, saliva flowing over my hands now, making it easier to stroke his base. "Squeeze me harder. Yeah, like that. You're going to kill me, baby."

At this point, I'm fairly confident I could tap my clit and make myself come. It's ridiculous how turned on I am, but it's not an exaggeration to say I could do this for hours. Happily. Sore jaw be damned.

Dar tilts my head back, forcing me to meet his eyes as the tip of his length hits the back of my throat, making me gag.

Neither of us pauses.

"I've thought about this so many times. So many fucking times. Thought I was a dirty old man, imagining a hot young thing on her knees for me. But you like it, don't you? Like knowing what you've done to me?"

What *I've* done to *him*? What about what he's done to *me*?

There's no coming back from this, no returning to normal sex with normal people who don't realize what I need before I've had time to figure it out myself. It feels wrong to even think about it.

In the back of my mind, I know I was ruined for anyone else long before tonight.

The taste of his pre-cum is flowing over my tongue now. I whimper as he takes control, dragging my head up and down, setting the pace he needs to finish this. "That's my girl. Rub your clit. I need you there with me." He spits each word through clenched teeth, and my hand drops between my thighs.

It's been ages since I came without the help of a vibrator, but within seconds I'm whimpering and shaking, unable to keep my eyes on Dar's face.

Without warning, he pulls me off him and takes over completely, jerking his cock with rough efficiency.

His cum hits my face in long streaks, painting my lips, my cheeks, and the tops of my breasts. I'm covered with him, and that's when I come too, writhing and moaning at Dar's feet, painted in his release and grinding desperately against my own fingers.

I've said *holy crap* a lot in my life, but *holy-actual-crap.*

"Savvy, baby." Seconds later, I'm being lifted off my knees and into the seat Dar was just occupying while he kneels in front of me. He steals a napkin from the table and cleans me, chest still rising and falling harder than normal.

Dar's hand falls back to his side, and for a moment, all we can do is stare at each other in stunned silence.

I'm not sure who does it first, or if we're still so deeply in sync that it happens as one, but suddenly, we're laughing. Peals of hysterical, breathless laughter fill the room, and tears stream from the corners of my eyes.

God, have I ever heard him laugh like this? Have I ever heard him laugh *ever*?

Then again, when's the last time I did? Not a reluctant giggle or chuckle, but big, full-body laughs that makes it hard to breathe and seem to go on forever. Not being able to remember probably means it's been a while.

When we've finally calmed down and my cheeks ache from smiling, Dar gets to his feet, tucking himself away.

I watch as he crosses the kitchen to gather up my cast-off clothes, then comes back to kneel at my feet.

"You're already sick of seeing me naked?" I tease gently, allowing him to slip my panties over my ankles and drag them back up my legs.

His stern answering look is so familiar, I can't help giggling. "Have mercy, little tornado. Let me feed you, then I'll strip you naked and take you to bed. Would you like that?"

He kisses the hollow between my breasts one more time before pulling my summer dress over my head.

I hum happily, lifting my arms through the holes obligingly. "Yes."

As he tugs the white cotton over my thighs, Dar glares at the material as if it offended him. "Did you wear this to drive all day?"

My stomach flips. I think I'm going to enjoy jealous Dar. Unfortunately, it's unnecessary right now. "No," I admit, curling my arms around the back of his neck, loving that I'm *allowed* to do that. "I stopped home before coming here. There may have been a frantic closet search that resulted in every article of clothing I own in a pile on the bed."

Dar kisses me, slow enough to make my heart flutter and hard enough to make me ache. When he pulls away, there's a shadow of worry in his eyes. "I'm sorry I couldn't... that I didn't touch you. I wanted to. Wanting to isn't the problem."

"I know," I assure him, playing with his hair.

It was scary to watch one of Dar's episodes happen in real time. I'd known it could happen, that *this*—being physically intimate—might take a while, but I couldn't have predicted how awful it would be to see the torment in his eyes.

"You kissed me, though, Dar. That's so big. You let me touch you... put my mouth on you." My skin prickles with heat, I'm not alone if the look I receive in return is anything to go by. It's a bit of a struggle to pick up my train of thought again. "Tonight wasn't a baby step. It was, like, a football field–sized leap. I was doing some research on supporting a loved one with OCD and—"

"Is that what I am to you?" Dar asks, cutting off my rambling. His thumb brushes over my bottom lip, those impossibly dark eyes boring into mine. "A loved one?"

He is, and I think he knows it too, but something sharp lodges in my chest when I go to say it.

Losing him once was impossible. How could I make it

through a second time when I finally know for sure that this connection wasn't all in my head? What if down the road he decides this—*us*—is more trouble than it's worth and calls the whole thing off?

No.

I take a deep breath, tearing myself from the mental spiral this conversation sent me into. Dar is trying. He's *more* than trying. He's changing his entire life to fit me into it, pushing himself to work past boundaries he's had for years, *for me*.

What more could I ask for?

It's time for me to be brave, and not in the wild, reckless way I always have, when I didn't really care about the consequences. This is different.

The crescendo is swelling to its final peak, the waves have crashed onto the beach, and I am leaning over the precipice of something I can't take back.

What happens next is out of my control. We are gravity.

Callused fingers skim the curve of my throat, raising goosebumps in their wake. Dar's eyes follow the motion, captivated, like he can't believe this is happening, that he's touching me. The awe in his face, the adoration…

"Yes." My stomach swoops as I answer the question, as though I really have just fallen, and my hands tighten on Dar's shoulders. "Always. Even when I didn't want you to be. Even when it hurt."

The words settle over us, and when Dar's eyes find mine again, they're shining with emotion I'm not sure I've ever seen before. The corner of his lips lift into a wry little smile. "Partners?"

I let out a startled laugh, my heart full to bursting as I nod. "Yes. Partners."

This time, we do better than a handshake.

CHAPTER 16
DARWIN

"OKAY, HOW DOES THIS LOOK?"

My head falls to the side, looking diligently up at the mounted TV Savvy is adjusting above the prize counter, or, at least, I'm *trying* to look diligently.

Admittedly, it's difficult to get my eyes to move past my girlfriend's ass, which is conveniently positioned at my eye level thanks to the ladder she's standing on.

"Dar," Savvy chides, and I force my gaze up to meet hers. I smile sheepishly, but my life feels better than I can remember it ever being. This woman… fuck. I never stood a chance.

"Sorry." I step back, shoving my hands in my pockets to— hopefully— disguise my erection. "It looks great. When did you have this idea?"

Along with the traditional arcade prizes, which range anywhere from stickers to a professional drone, Savvy thought it would be a good idea to offer players the option to trade in their ticket winnings for food from the snack bar or rounds of laser tag. It's all advertised on the digital sign she's spent the better part of an hour setting up.

"Last night," she replies, shooting a little smirk over her shoulder, eyes sparkling.

My heart stalls. Fuck, she's so beautiful. Is it too soon to propose?

"I wasn't aware you had *time* to think about our business last night."

After a day spent finishing up odd tasks around here, I brought her home with me. Just like we've done every day for a week, and just like I intend to do as often as possible.

Forever, if I can manage it.

"I'm very good at multitasking," my little tornado says primly, turning back to fiddle with the remote control. The little tease moves one foot up a step, accentuating her perfect ass. Recent experience has taught me there's a zero percent chance this was accidental.

"Apparently." I stroll around the counter, hands still in my pockets. "Work-life balance is very important, Savvy. Would tying you to our bed and making you come until you pass out take your mind off things?"

It's big talk from a man who still hasn't been able to do that, but Savvy turns so quickly the ladder wobbles. My foot finds the bottom step, pressing it down before she topples off, and I lift my hands to her hips.

"Dar!" She giggles, unperturbed by how close we came to spending our evening in the emergency room instead. "The kids are here."

"The kids are painting the birthday party space. They're occupied." I lean forward and sink my teeth into the swell of her ass, biting playfully through her little shorts.

Above me, there's a ragged gasp that's almost immediately drowned out by a loud exclamation of "gross" from the doorway to the arcade.

We both whip around to find Marley standing just inside the room, glaring at us with her nose wrinkled in disgust.

"Can you guys, like, *not* be so into each other? Old people shouldn't be this thirsty. It's embarrassing."

I pinch the bridge of my nose while, above me, Savvy bursts into laughter. "Can we help you, Marley?"

"Yeah, can we order Chinese for dinner?"

"Go for it," I tell her wryly, reaching into my back pocket for my credit card. "Get extra egg rolls this time."

When she's gone, Savvy climbs down and twines her arms behind my neck. "You're so cute with them. Like a nerdy, sarcastic mama duck."

"The little shits have grown on me." I drag her closer. "Do you want kids?"

Savvy bites her lip. "With the right person, yeah, I think so. I hated going back and forth between my parents' houses though. So I'd want to be, like, two hundred percent sure about my partner."

My heart lurches, and I lean down to capture her lips in a kiss that's too intense to be played off as anything other than a desperate bid to make it clear *I* intend to be that person. When we part, panting, Savvy smiles mischievously. "What about you? What's your stance on making small humans?"

Just imagining Savvy pregnant with my child is enough to knock the wind out of me. The possibility of having a family of my own was unthinkable for so long that it's startling to realize how badly I want it now.

I swallow back the sudden burst of longing. "Pro. Definitely, pro."

Another kiss, this time more heated than the last, but Savvy ends it quickly, letting her head drop back with a frustrated little groan. "You're making me so wet. We have to stop."

I don't want to stop. I want to lock us in the back office and worship her beautiful pussy with my fingers, tongue, and cock in no particular order. We've been... intimate, but the reality that I still haven't made her come has become a source of near-constant frustration for me. Since our first date, the level of dumb lust has risen to unbearable levels. We can barely keep our hands off each other, but I haven't tried to push it further. The memory of my panic when it came time to touch her... I can't do that again. To either of us. I have to make sure, but I have no idea *how*.

I even broached the subject with Doctor Lucas at our appointment this morning, but the unhelpful asshole was more focused on unpacking how I *felt* about the whole situation than on telling me how to solve it. Savvy's constant reassurances that she doesn't mind taking it slow only make me feel worse.

She might not mind, but I sure as hell do.

"Dar." Warm hands touch my face, and I blink down at Savvy, realizing I've been staring off into space.

"Sorry." I kiss her forehead. "I came over to talk to you about something. Your ass distracted me."

She smirks. "I'm not going to apologize for that."

I chuckle. "Nor should you. Anyway, the show's production team and a good portion of the cast will be in New York this weekend for some gala, and my agent suggested we set up a meeting while they're so close. I suspect she thinks there's a better likelihood of me agreeing if I don't have to get on a plane."

A slow, excited smile is curling over Savvy's face. "You're going?"

"Not if you need me here. It's very last minute, and Patricia is used to me telling her no."

"Everything is under control. You should absolutely go." She moves to wrap her arms around me, but a second later, as if something's just occurred to her, she stops and glares up at me. "As long as you promise not to leave me for a movie star."

It's probably wrong to be smug, but I can't help it. I love that she's as possessive of me as I am of her.

Tugging playfully on a lock of her hair, I laugh. "Unless they have pink hair and can kick my ass at Mario Kart, they're not my type."

I kiss her one more time, but when I draw away, intending to finish updating the point-of-sale system, Savvy's hands tighten on my shirt, stopping me.

The little smirk she's wearing has me abandoning all thoughts of productivity. "Do you want to play a game later?"

My mouth is suddenly bone dry. "A game?"

Savvy nods, running her hands down my chest to hook two fingers through the belt loops on my jeans. "Later. After the kids have gone home for the night."

"What kind of game?"

Her smile widens, and the mischievous glint in her eye might be the sexiest, most terrifying thing I've ever seen. "Laser tag."

———

When I return to Galactic Guild, the lobby is dark and quiet. Savvy closed everything down for the night while I was dropping the kids off, and now, the only lights are shining from between the big, swinging doors that lead into the laser tag briefing room.

Savvy finished laying the new flooring a few days ago, and my shoes squeak as I cross the room, anticipation moving farther up my spine with each step. This could just be an innocent game, her way of taking my mind off things, but I know it won't be.

I know my girlfriend—I still get a thrill whenever I think of her in that context—would never be so predictable. Where my brain works in controlled, methodical steps, always considering every possible scenario, Savvy is the opposite. As situations arise, she handles them. Foresight is hardly her greatest strength, but I've never met anyone with such a knack for pulling ideas out of thin air.

Is it strange to be attracted to someone's mind? Because I am.

All questions about what is or isn't normal vanish as I push open the door.

The room is lit by unearthly blue light, illuminating the rows of benches to my right and hooks of vests and laser guns hung on charging mounts to my left. In the center of the room is Savvy.

She's wearing the same infuriatingly sexy shorts as earlier, but has discarded her T-shirt, leaving her top half covered only by a sports bra and black laser tag vest. A braid of pink hair is hanging over her shoulder.

"Hi." Savvy smirks, shifting her weight to show off the holster strapped around her bare thigh, laser gun inside.

I can barely swallow. "You look incredible."

Her eyes sparkle in the neon light. "Do I? Thank you."

"I think I should be the one thanking you right now." As I move forward to touch her, though, Savvy steps away, her smile widening. Wordlessly, she gestures to a vest and gun laid out on one of the benches.

"We're playing a game, remember?"

Alright. I'll bite.

I feel her eyes on me as I pull the vest over my head. It's not heavy or bulky, but the large, flat LED lights on the front and back make it oddly stiff.

Not unlike my cock, which has been violently hard since I walked in here and found her in that fucking outfit.

"I've been thinking," Savvy says coyly, and I can tell my little tornado is loving this. "We've both been way too in our heads. About the sex thing." Hearing the word "sex" come out of her mouth while she's dressed like that is the equivalent of waving a red flag in front of a bull. All I want is to charge across the room, throw her over my shoulder, and do whatever it takes to make her come.

She wants to play with me, though, and I want to give her whatever she wants.

I pick up the gun. "Have we?"

"Mhmm," she hums, flicking her braid back. "That doesn't matter right now. I have a high-stakes mission for you, Commander Wilder. Should you choose to accept it."

This is a scene in one of my books.

Fucking hell, she has my dick so hard. I love seeing her like this—playful, confident and sexy, a woman who *knows* she's making my blood boil just by breathing. How the hell did I get so lucky?

I clear my throat, endeavoring to keep my shit together, to play along. "What's the mission?"

She moves toward me, stopping when we're toe to toe, her smile widening. "It's simple, Commander. You need to find and capture the rebel by any means necessary."

Christ.

My mouth goes dry as I nod. "I accept." And, unable to resist touching her when she's so close, I curl my free hand around the back of her neck, dragging her into me. The plastic on our vests bumps together noisily, and Savvy giggles, her warm hands settling on my shoulders. "What happens when I capture the rebel?"

"You're awfully confident, Commander." "Well, I did write the book on this."

Her answering laugh makes me feel ten feet tall.

"Well, then, I'm sure you know. Don't be afraid to go… off book, though." I lean in to kiss her, but Savvy is already moving away, shooting me one last teasing smile.

My cock throbs when she turns to the tablet mounted beside the arena doors, allowing me an incredible view of her ass in those shorts. A moment later, the lights on our vests and guns come to life, glowing for a few seconds before fading. Beyond the double doors, music starts.

Savvy reaches down, removing her gun from its holster. "Ten hits and you're out of luck, Commander." Before I can even think to respond or shake off the fog of desire she has me in, Savvy's gun is raised and the light on my vest is flashing pink. She beams. "That's one."

Then, we're moving.

The door to the arena has barely begun closing behind Savvy before I'm shoving it open, looking wildly around, but she's already vanished.

It's like I've stepped into another world. Stone was so into this shit, constantly finding ways to add new features, building spacecraft wreckage or installing the machine that creates the white smoke curling around my knees.

The pathway through the arena is lit by strips of LED lights, dimmed so they don't detract from the fantasy of it all, and above my head, strobing, technicolor laser beams give the illusion of an intense battle underway. The low beat of the electronic music settles deep in my chest, as though it's pulsing in time with my own heart.

Fuck me, there's something so intoxicating about the possibility of letting go and surrendering myself to this. It would be easy. Savvy knew it too. She figured out I needed to get out of my own fucking head.

So, without wasting another second, I do.

Prowling forward on the balls of my feet, I duck through a cave illuminated by strobing green lights, heading for a small bridge at the edge of the arena. My little tornado might know me, but I know her too, and that she loves the element of surprise. My bet is that she'll be lurking in the structures bordering the largest center tower, waiting to ambush me when I use it for a better vantage point.

I don't need to see the whole arena, though. I just need a clear view of the base of the tower.

Sure enough, when I edge along the side of the bridge, staring out at the area where I expect her to be, movement in the shadow of a towering pile of faux galactic waste crates makes my heart leap.

I wait, straining my eyes through the black light to confirm, but the angle is wrong. It doesn't matter. She's there.

I take the stairs back down to ground level two at a time, flat out running toward where I saw her, gun held aloft.

My pace only slows when the crates are in sight. She might have moved on already, correcting course when I didn't immediately go for the tower. I'm prepared for that, but I edge around the corner just in time to see a flash of bright pink rounding the crates ahead.

I follow.

My heart is thundering in my chest, but my movements are calm and measured. I'm a hunter, and she's my prey. This game we're playing is as old as time, and I'm about to win.

There's no need to rush this.

My eyes find her the moment I turn the next corner. Savvy is six feet away with her back to me, peeking around a pillar with her gun held close to her chest. She's focused on the tower, and with the deep thudding rhythm of the song playing, it's unlikely she'll be able to hear my footsteps.

She doesn't.

Still, my little tornado—*my rebel*—seems to sense she's being watched. I'm three feet away when I see her shoulders stiffen, but when she begins to turn, it's already too late.

The flashing lights on her vest are the only warning she gets before I lunge, pulling her back into my chest roughly, and I hear her gasp even over the pulsing beat of the music.

Our guns clatter to the ground.

"Hello, Commander." Her laugh is breathy as I reach down, tearing at the strap of her vest. It gives way, and I shove it away impatiently, squeezing her pierced tits through her sports bra while my other hand makes its way to her throat.

"Is this what you wanted?" I grit out, my lips brushing the shell of her ear. Savvy whimpers, her pulse racing under my touch. With no true effort, she struggles against my hold, trying to get away, and my fingers tighten on her throat. "Does this turn you on? Let's check."

I shove my hand down the front of those fucking shorts. If I wasn't out of control before, feeling the soft, wet skin of her cunt would decimate whatever rational thought processes I had left.

Holy fuck, she's so wet.

We're acting on instinct, desperate creatures rubbing against each other in a dark corner because *we need this*.

I ease two fingers through her slit, and my body shakes with hers when they brush over her swollen clit, stroking in gentle circles.

She bucks into my touch greedily, and my hold on her throat tightens. "Is all this for me?" I rasp, and the helpless little whimper I get in response makes my stiff cock ache.

My fingers push farther down, searching for her entrance. My eyes squeeze shut as I push inside her for the first time, feeling the impossibly hot, tight walls of her cunt.

"Holy shit—*holy fucking shit*—baby, you're so goddamn tight."

I'm barely aware of what I'm saying, too focused on cataloging Savvy's reactions to all this. She's getting slicker with each word, and I feel a surge of triumph because even without having done this before, I know what my girl likes.

I know how to make her wet.

We stumble forward, and the front of Savvy's legs hit one of the crates of toxic waste.

"I'm going to fuck you bare," I warn, grinding my palm over her clit as I work my fingers in and out, getting her ready. "Do you want my cum inside you, baby?"

My fingers curve, searching, and I know I've hit the good spot when Savvy's legs almost buckle.

"Dar! Oh fuck, *please*!" She's shaking in my arms, rubbing against my hand the best she can, looking for relief.

"Come for me." My voice is so rough, I barely recognize it. "Come on my fingers. Give it to me, and then I'll fuck you nice and hard. You want it that way, don't you? Want to feel this slick little hole being used the way it's meant to be?"

There have been a handful of moments in my life when I thought I felt victorious. When I finished my first book. When I signed that first publishing contract. When I kissed Savvy for the first time. All those times were incredible, life-affirming even, but none of them compare to making her come apart on my fingers.

Flashing lights and deep, pulsing music carry through the arena around us, but I'm hardly aware of any of it. All I can do is watch, bewitched, as Savvy's lips part, her face transformed by the pleasure I'm giving her as her inner walls clamp down.

Fuck. Yes.

Her body has barely stopped writhing against mine before I have her bent over, peeling those skin tight shorts down her legs and leaving them tangled around her ankles.

I'd like to stop and admire her, to touch every inch of her beautiful body, but there's no way I can take this slow. My cock is harder than iron and leaking so much pre-cum that it's soaked through my boxers. Urgency is humming under my skin, demanding I do this now. Fill her. Own her. Make her mine.

No more waiting.

My hands are steady as I reach for my belt and fly, undoing them to allow my cock to spring free. It's not a relief. The ache is still so intense, it makes my teeth ache.

Savvy manages to free one ankle from her shorts and, still

bent over the crate, she lifts her leg onto the surface too, offering herself up to me.

My breath comes in ragged pants as I grip my base, guiding the tip through her slit, coating it with the same wetness still sticky on my fingers. The flashing lights above us give everything an oddly surreal quality, but we're not in a fantasy. This is real, it's happening, and I *need* to see her face when it does.

"Dar," Savvy gasps, and as I press my tip against her intensely narrow entrance, my eyes lift to meet hers. A silent understanding passes between us, and I didn't know it was possible to feel this connected to another person. There's no hesitation, no self-consciousness or fear. Only a bone-deep need that must be satisfied by the other.

My free hand finds her hip, anchoring us together, and that's the last conscious decision I make.

A rough noise leaves my chest as I press forward into heaven. Nothing has ever felt better than this, and I suspect nothing ever will. She was made for me, her hot, wet walls gripping my cock like a fucking sleeve. The world doesn't exist beyond the two of us, and I don't stop until my balls are pressed against her clit, the head of my cock hitting the deepest part of her and—*holy fuck*. I have to bite my tongue to stop myself from coming in one thrust.

Savvy is clawing at the crate, peeking back at me with a shocked, hot-as-fuck look on her face. "Dar, Dar, Dar," she chants, spreading her legs wider to offer me more.

I take it.

As I pull back, my eyes fall to the space between us, watching as her little cunt clings to my too-big-for-her cock. I'm addicted. I want to see this every day for the rest of my life. Now that I know how fucking incredible it feels to be inside this woman, I'll never be able to stop.

It doesn't take long for my pace to become savage. Each thrust is sharp and rough, each withdrawal slow and lingering, sending Savvy to the tips of her toes. And when the music changes, I can hear the sexy-as-hell cries that leave her lips when I hit bottom, a noise somewhere between pain and pleasure.

"*Oh god.* Fuck, Dar!" She's babbling now, almost sobbing as I begin to pick up speed.

She's close, and I need to get her there before I lose it completely. Lunging forward, I press my lips to the back of her damp neck, shoving my hand beneath her to rub furiously over the stiff nub between her legs. "You were made to take my dick, weren't you, baby? You fit me just right."

Savvy lips part, her moans lost to the swelling music. I'm going at her hard, but my little tornado takes all of it, arching her back to let me deeper as the connection between us swells to something all consuming and inescapable.

I took her. She's mine, and I'm not giving her back.

My abs are burning, my thighs aching, but the pleasure building at the base of my spine has become unbearable, and I can't slow down. This won't last much longer and, desperate now, I pinch her throbbing clit. "Come," I snarl. "Fucking come, baby."

Her walls clamp down, clutching at my shaft as Savvy's body shakes with the force of her orgasm, the sound of her cries muffled.

My beautiful, fearless girl, my personal miracle, coming undone beneath me—*because of me.* It's too intense, too much, and the frayed tether of my control breaks.

I come, filling her with my release and cementing the primal, possessive feeling that's settled deep inside me.

We collapse over the crate, undignified and damp with sweat, me fully dressed—laser tag vest still in place—and her bare apart from a sports bra and her shorts tangled around one ankle.

"*Baby.*" I half groan, half laugh, so fucking elated I could burst.

Savvy turns, resting her head on her arm and beaming at me. "Why am I 'baby' when I'm naked but 'little tornado' the rest of the time?" she teases, lifting a hand to play with my beard.

"Too many syllables."

Her laughter carries over the music, and I find myself annoyed by our current location. "Come on." I stand, re-fastening my pants, then kneel at Savvy's feet to help her pull her panties and shorts back up.

"Where are we going now, Commander Wilder?" she questions once I've retrieved the dropped laser tag equipment and taken her hand, leading the way out of the arena.

Fake smoke curls around our ankles, and flickering lights shine on Savvy's golden skin. Maybe I should feel guilty about this, or at least conflicted for fucking my dead friend's daughter in the place he once loved most in the world, but I don't.

It's hers now—ours—and I won't hold myself back from her for anything or anyone.

My thumb brushes over Savvy's hand, already so familiar in mine. "I'm taking you home."

To Do: ⭐

~~Find a realtor for GG~~

~~Meeting with accountant~~

~~Find an accountant~~

Exact revenge on Caleb

~~Clean literally everything~~

Fix literally everything

~~Talk to HIM~~

~~New Vacuum~~

~~Rip up stained carpet in lobby + snackbar~~

~~Replace those long lightbulbs in the ceiling~~

~~Find out which games in arcade don't work~~

~~Fix roof leak~~

~~Reconnect security system (at some point)~~

Find a therapist

~~Figure out why my car is making that clanky noise~~

~~New bathroom light fixture~~

~~Research competitor pricing~~

~~Complete the Google Ads course~~

~~Locate source of weird smell in back hallway~~

~~Buy tampons!!!!!!!!~~

~~Finish new website~~

~~Create social media graphics for Laser Speed Dating~~

~~Start ads on b-day parties~~

Get a ~~bikini wax~~ like now

Train kids on new POS system

Kids paint B-day rooms

Stock arcade games

Stock snack bar

Update business hours

CHAPTER 17
SAVVY

S O, here's the thing: laser tag isn't generally considered a very sexy activity.

I get it. Scrambling around a dark room with a bunch of screaming kids brandishing laser guns, wearing the same sweaty vest as god knows how many other people, isn't an aphrodisiac. There's always someone monitoring the games too, poised to hit the dreaded penalty button if you lay a finger on another player. Laser tag is strictly no contact, or, at least, it's supposed to be.

Except last night, when Dar and I broke *all* the rules.

We were both exhausted by the time we made it back to his house after leaving the arena, but still found the energy to make slow, sleepy love against the shower wall, hot water pooling between our bodies as he made me come not once, not twice, but three times before finishing deep inside me.

Love making.

I always thought that term was sentimental and cheesy, but I don't know what else to call what happened between us in the shower. It wasn't rough or frantic, nothing like the combustion of weeks of need that our first time was. I clung to his shoulders, our quiet noises of pleasure echoing off the walls of the glass shower, kissing until we were too far gone to do more than pant and moan.

After all that, my heart feels *changed*. If there was any doubt in my mind that I'm not completely in love with Darwin Wilder, it's gone now. Even if I'm annoyed that the big jerk would hit me with the best sex of my life, then take off for twenty-four hours.

This morning, the production company sent a fancy black town car for Dar to take him into the city, and I kissed him goodbye at the door wearing nothing but a t-shirt I stole from his drawer. He got halfway down the path before abruptly turning around, marching back up to the house and silencing my question of whether he'd forgotten something with a frantic, searing kiss.

A few hours later, I floated into Galactic Guild with cartoon hearts in my eyes and a cloud of pink birds circling my head. Even now, with half the day gone, I still get all fluttery and weak-kneed whenever I think about it.

I'm in so much trouble.

All day I've been fending off daydreams of matching wedding bands and grumpy, dark-haired babies. Then again, considering he came inside me *twice* without questioning my birth control methods, Dar doesn't seem to be any better.

"Your face looks weird." I blink, pulled from my preoccupation by King. He's standing on the other side of the snack bar, which I'm still using as my office, with a broom in hand and his nose scrunched up.

"I'm your boss. It's in your best interest to lie to me when that's the case," I advise, tapping my pencil on the glass countertop.

"Honesty's the best policy, Savvy!" sings Marley as she comes into view, Luke at her heels. "What do you need us to do now?"

I pause, glancing around, and my heart lifts when it occurs to me how much *doesn't* need to be done. There are still plenty of things I'd like to change or improve when money starts coming in, but Galactic Guild feels fresh. A lot of the original character remains in the murals and the old-school games, but there's new paint on the walls, and the stained purple carpet has been replaced with wood.

Now, I'm confident that people won't be afraid they're sending their kids into a possible crime scene anymore, and— holy shit. *I* did this. Me. Dar helped so much, but it was my vision, my plans. We're officially opening in one week, and I'm excited. People are already booking birthday parties on the new website, and I announced the first Laser Speed Dating event this morning on our social media accounts.

Biting back a smile, I send the kids off to begin stocking all the claw machines in the arcade, then pick up my phone.

> Savvy: Hey, this is your daily reminder that I love you, and I'm ready to talk whenever you are.

> Raven: *Insert middle finger emoji that was unfairly taken away here*

I sigh, staring down at the string of text exchanges from the last few days, which have all been pretty much the same.

She'll get over it. We've fought in the past, and Raven's always needed a few weeks to simmer off before she's ready to admit she might have been even a tiny bit wrong about something. She's protective of me, and I get that, but she needs to trust that I'm not going into this with my eyes closed.

My heart flutters as I cross my legs and feel *that* ache again. Biting my lip, I type out another text.

> Savvy: How's it going? Have you met the cast yet?

Dar: I'm just heading there now. Had a sit down with the production team and was overall impressed. They're cutting a few scenes I'd rather they didn't. We'll see.

Savvy: That's why the book is ALWAYS better.

Dar: I miss you. Going in now. I'll call you before bed?

Savvy: Yes, please.

Grinning like a hormone-drunk lunatic, I open my laptop, and—almost instantly—my jaw drops.

The Galactic Guild Arena Instagram, which had about thirty followers this morning, has leapt to over five thousand. There are hundreds of notifications, but all of them seem to be on the Laser Speed Dating post.

Even as I watch, more comments are popping up, all of them asking when another one will be, tagging their friends, complaining about tickets being sold out, or just saying what a cool, fun idea it is. There's a message from an event coordinator at a local radio station asking if we would be interested in co-hosting an event.

My hands are shaky as I click over to our website. Sure enough, the event sold out in about ten minutes.

I know I should start responding to all these messages or looking at our calendar to get more events on the books, but I've never felt like this before… Like I might not be such a failure after all, and there's only one person I *need* to tell about it.

> Savvy: You won't get this for a while, but the post announcing Laser Speed Dating went kind of viral… We're sold out, and all our accounts have thousands of new followers. A radio station DMed me about an event!

I've barely set my phone down, though, when his response comes.

> Dar: I'm so fucking proud of you, little tornado. I told you it was brilliant!

Wiping my eyes impatiently, I beam down at the phone.

> Savvy: Aren't you with movie stars right now?!

> Dar: I don't give a damn who I'm with, Savvy. When you text me, I'm going to respond.

Even though I'm having the greatest morning ever recorded, I consider my greatest victory of the day to be not sliding off my stool and melting into a puddle on the spot.

Darwin Wilder, the reclusive grump, has somehow transformed himself into the sweetest boyfriend ever in a matter of weeks.

Who would have thought?

Not me, that's for sure. Even in my wildest fantasies, being with Dar wasn't like this, and suddenly all those stupid *when you know, you know* pearls of wisdom kind of make sense. Because *I freaking know.* I am going to marry that big, grumpy nerd and have his oversized, grumpy, nerdy babies (sorry vagina), and that's that.

I'm sold, and it's terrifying.

It takes my heart a solid thirty seconds to regain its normal rhythm and my brain to focus on anything other than the man I'm so clearly in love with. But when I finally turn back to my work, my computer yields its second surprise of the day.

An application update pops up in the right corner of my screen, and I stare at the unfamiliar icon, trying to remember what the hell it's for.

Then, it hits me.

It's the software Dar installed so we can monitor Galactic Guild remotely, set the alarms or—a hysterical little giggle bubbles from my lips—review security footage. As in…

My face is hot as I peer over my computer screen to where Marley, King, and Luke are busy filling claw machines with little prizes, oblivious to the fact that their boss may or may not be about to find a video of herself being fucked by their other boss.

I feel like a voyeur as I open the software and start clicking through the footage, like I'm searching for someone else's possible sex tape and not my own. There are dozens of cameras in the arena, but it's huge in there. The chances there is one exactly where we—My heart stalls. *There it is.* A camera is directed right on that *very* familiar galactic waste pile, and there's just one motion-activated recording on that day.

Heart pounding, I skip forward, finally stopping on a frame of myself just as I step into the camera's path. The footage is crystal clear, and I can see my sly smile as I creep further into view, looking back and forth, laser gun clutched in my hands.

I'm only alone for a few seconds.

I know what's going to happen, but my heart still jolts when a dark figure appears out of nowhere, grabbing me… I snap the computer shut.

Later. I'll watch it later.

———

It's later. Finally.

Normally with the craziness of getting Galactic Guild up and running, in between lusting after Dar and squeezing in a rideshare shift whenever I can, I'm too busy for the days to drag. Today, though, I couldn't stop checking the time, waiting for the end of the kids' shift so I could go home too.

My phone is password protected, but I still didn't let it out of my sight. The knowledge of what it contained, and that I'd deleted the only other copy of the footage, kept me from my usual routine of leaving it some obscure corner of Galactic Guild and needing help to hunt it down.

After driving King, Marley, and Luke back into town to meet their friends—ignoring their mutinous grumbling that I hadn't fed them dinner like Dar always does—I drove straight home, gripping the wheel like my life depended on it.

Kicking my sandals off in the entryway (beside the other jumble of discarded shoes), I jog up the steps to the main floor, snag an apple from the bag on the table, and stride right down the dark hall to my bedroom.

The space hasn't changed a lot since my teenage years. Even my old clothes are crammed into bins in the closet, waiting for the day when I get around to donating them. It couldn't be clearer that I never intended for this to be a permanent arrangement.

Maybe it won't be.

If things with Dar are as serious as they feel... I don't let myself linger on that for long. Truthfully, living in his fortress of solitude doesn't sound a lot better than staying here. One step at a time, though. Right now, I want to watch myself have crazy laser tag sex with my boyfriend, whom I liked *before* falling under his dick spell.

Wriggling out of my clothes, I toss them in the general direction of my hamper and flop onto the unmade bed, giggling at my own enthusiasm. There is no earthly reason for me to feel so naughty watching this—it's *me* having sex for god's sake—but I can't wipe the mischievous smile off my face.

The moment I start the video, all humor is forgotten.

Watching porn has never really been my thing, but this is different. It's me and Dar, and seeing the uncontrolled, desperate way he holds me, strips me, uses me… by the time it's finished, I'm sopping wet and reaching blindly for the vibrator in my bedside table.

My hands fumble as I situate the pink device over my clit and restart the video. I'm already so worked up, I only make it to the part where Dar hunches forward over me, his handsome face lost in pleasure, before my body bows off the bed and I come with a broken cry.

Wow. I will never delete this video. Ever. I'll have to be careful with it, because Dar is a semi-public figure and I'm sure there are some sci-fi fans out there who would love to see the man naked (I know because I was one of them), but this is non-negotiable.

I'm considering a third viewing when the phone rings, and my heart leaps at the sight of the name on the caller ID.

"Hey," I breathe, sinking back into my pillows. "It's late. Are you just getting back to your hotel?"

He sighs, like he's relieved to hear my voice. "I am. How are you?

How's everything there?"

I roll over onto my side, smiling. "Good. Really good. I scheduled four more events for next month, and they're already sold out. The radio show looks like it will happen too. We're going to need to hire people, Dar! I can't run this place by myself, and your baby ducks go back to school in the fall."

Dar laughs quietly. "I'm not even slightly surprised. You're a force of nature, little tornado."

It's impossible to stop the big, ridiculous smile from spreading over my face. "Tell me about meeting the cast. Is Noa Lowell that pretty in person?"

"This feels like a trap."

I giggle. "No, seriously. Were they nice? I've always wondered."

"You'll meet them for yourself, and you can decide."

"What? No, I won't."

"You will. Now that Patricia's seen I'm willing to leave the house, the woman won't let anything rest." He's trying his best to sound annoyed, but I can tell he's proud of himself. "I let her manipulate me into agreeing to attend the season one premier."

My mouth falls open. "Seriously? Like, with the red carpet and everything? I get to wear a fancy, sparkly dress?"

His chuckle makes me feel warm all over. "I'll buy you the fanciest, sparkliest dress. They won't be able to get a single decent picture of us because the camera flashes will reflect off you."

"I—" My eyes burn, and I have to press my lips together to keep myself from blurting out the words that immediately come to mind. *I love you.* God, I really, really do, but this isn't the time. "I'm really proud of you," I say instead, and it's just as true. "You're amazing the way you are, though. Don't feel like you have to become this whole other person or do things that don't make you happy just to please me."

"I don't," he assures me smoothly. "This is my story. I spent more than half my life writing it, and now it's going to reach even more people. It's important for me to see it through." There's a pause. "Also, I can *please you* without leaving the house, Miss Laurence."

"Is that a sex joke, Mr. Wilder?"

"If you have to ask, it's not a very good one."

I grin, flopping onto my back. "Maybe you can show me what you had in mind when you get home." My fingers trail over my bare stomach.

Through the phone, I hear Dar exhale. "I want to be inside you right now."

Heat settles between my legs, and I'm sure he can hear the way his words make my breath catch. I'm tempted to take this further, to make him listen while I come with his name on my lips, but this opportunity is too good to pass up. "I'll make sure to skip the panties tomorrow, but I have something to get you through the night."

"I doubt that," comes Dar's rough reply, and I snicker. "I'm going to bed. I'll send it to you before I do, though." He groans. "Fuck, baby."

"See you in the morning," I sing teasingly, then end the call.

I'm almost giddy as I pull up the video and send it to him. It's more than a little hot to think about Dar laying on his hotel room bed, making himself come as he watches us, the same way I did.

Though, admittedly, not as hot as the thought of what he's going to do to me tomorrow.

CHAPTER 18
SAVVY

'VE NEVER BEEN the type to have trouble sleeping. Ordinarily, I pass out and wake up eight (or ten) hours later, no meditating, pharmaceuticals, or sound machines required.

So, when I open my eyes to find the sky still dark outside my window, my brain takes a moment to come online. I lift my head, blinking hazily around at my silent bedroom as I try to figure out what woke me.

Then, I hear it.

Heavy footsteps on the carpeted stairs.

Instantly, I'm scrambling back against my headboard, a scream building in my throat. What do people do when there's an intruder in their house? Is that something I'm supposed to know? Why don't I keep a baseball bat next to my bed like in the movies? Should I try to call the police?

Before I can even reach for my phone, however, the door swings open and my intruder hits the lights, almost blinding me with the sudden brightness.

"Dar?" I shriek as I recognize the figure in the doorway, pressing my hands over my thundering heart.

He doesn't look the least bit repentant for making me believe I was about to be murdered. The jerk just stands there in the doorway, dressed in the same dark blazer and white button-up shirt he left the house in, glowering down at me.

"What are you doing here—*wait*, how did you get in?"

"I broke one of the window panes beside the door," he replies calmly, shrugging his blazer off and tossing atop my pink dresser with heart-shaped knobs.

I gape at him. "You broke into my house at"—I glance at the alarm clock—"*two thirty in the morning?*"

Dar's fingers move to the buttons of his shirt as he toes off the black leather shoes I helped him select in his closet yesterday. Before I found out he was a complete lunatic.

His lip curls. "I just spent three hours in a rideshare with a driver named *Toby*. During this time, I heard all about his relationship with his mother, the best method for cooking *corn-flavored popcorn*, why he's thinking of suing Netflix for stealing his idea for *The* fucking *Crown*, and was asked if I knew any *biddies* I could set him up with no less than four times."

I splutter as the shirt joins his blazer on the dresser, still trying to comprehend what the hell is going on. "You weren't supposed to be here until almost lunch!"

The belt goes next. "Take off your goddamn clothes, Savvy." His voice is deathly calm and authoritative. Did I just step into the principal's office?

"I—" I look down at the outline of my body beneath the sheets, then blink up at him again. "What?"

"*Now.*"

Shaking my head, I pull back the sheet. "I like to sleep naked." I press my thighs together, gazing up at the dark, hungry look on his face.

Oh boy. Should I be finding this hot? Because it might be kind of hot.

Without another word, Dar reaches behind his head to remove his white T-shirt, tossing it to the floor and striding right to the end of my bed. I barely have time to appreciate the sight of him shirtless, wearing only a pair of low-slung dress pants, before he leans forward to grab each of my ankles, and *pulls*.

I squeak as my butt is dragged to the edge of the mattress. Dar moves between my legs, his gaze raking over my naked body spread open and exposed for him.

Goosebumps erupt over my arms and down my back.

"Dar," I whine, and the fear and confusion I was filled with only a few seconds ago are ancient history. Future Savvy can get mad at him for scaring me to death. That's her problem. At the moment, I'm experiencing a swift shift in priorities.

He doesn't respond. Instead, with one last searing look up at me, Dar drops to his knees. "Eyes on me, little tornado. Watch me get a taste of my new favorite meal."

My lips part, intending to say… something? It doesn't matter. Nothing else matters, except the tall, dark-haired man between my legs and the way his hands tighten on the insides of my knees, holding me open so he can surge forward, sealing his mouth over my pussy. "Oh my god…" I gasp, already struggling to hold myself up, to watch like he told me to.

He's so… *into it.*

Every time I whimper or twitch, Dar redoubles his efforts, groaning like my pleasure is his own. The crude, wet noises that he makes as he laps at my clit seem to settle in my bones. His enjoyment makes this ten times hotter, and when I reach down to wind my fingers through his hair, dragging him closer, he actually growls.

Part of me wonders if this is a dream, because nobody has ever touched me like this before. Ever. It's hardly the first time I've had a man go down on me, but I always felt self-conscious, too worried that he wouldn't like something about this to properly enjoy it.

Dar's obvious enjoyment leaves no room for any of that now.

Two fingers find my entrance, curling to find my G-spot while he zeros in on my clit, alternating between sucking and teasing licks.

Dark eyes meet mine, and I gasp, my belly beginning to tighten.

"Dar!" I've lost the ability to say words other than his name, or maybe I just don't want to. He's everything and everywhere, working his tongue through my sex so hungrily, it's like he'll die if I don't come.

The elbow supporting me gives up the fight, and I fall flat on my back, my body shaking with the force of what he's pulling from me. I'm right there, chest heaving and both hands now tightening in Dar's hair. Mindless of anything but the need to come, I buck against his mouth, instinctively trying to get closer to the source of my pleasure.

Then, without warning, he's gone.

I cry out, looking up in time to see Dar roll back to his feet, letting my legs fall off the end of the bed. "I was so close!" There are actual tears of frustration in my eyes as I sit up, my thighs still spread.

"I'm aware." Long fingers, still coated with my arousal, move to the button on his pants. My eyes catch on the intimidating ridge of his erection, which is straining violently against the material. "I think you'll agree you deserved that, you little tease." I'm about to protest this, but then his pants and boxers go as one, kicked off toward the corner.

Darwin Wilder is naked and scowling down at me in the same bedroom where I once doodled *Mrs. Savvy Wilder* on my notebooks and anxiously applied cherry Lip Smackers before going to his house for dinner. There's a dusty, incomplete collection of his books on the shelf, and a miniature, glowing diagram of the moon, which he gave me for my thirteenth birthday, displayed beside the pinch-pot mug I made in ceramics class.

Evidence of my adolescent crush is everywhere, and now I'm a grown woman, aching for the same man as his saliva cools on my inner thighs.

My tongue darts out to wet my lips as Dar kneels on the edge of the bed. We move as one toward the center, my legs parting to make room for him. "I have a lot of frustration to burn off, baby," he coos, leaning down to brush his lips over mine. "You'll take it for me, won't you? You'll let me pound you into this mattress?"

The whimper I make in response must be sufficient, because Dar reaches between us, keeping his eyes on mine as he guides the head of his cock to my tender opening.

"*Damnit.*" He hisses as the first few inches of his length breach me. "There it is. Fuck, baby, you have no idea what you've done to me. The shit I want to do to you—"

My hands find his butt, pulling him deeper and helping him work his cock into me as our ragged breathing fills the bedroom. I'm never going to get used to feeling this full, there's no way. "Tell me," I plead, desperate to hear the effect I have on him, but my words turn to a scream as Dar drives forward, burying himself completely in a single thrust that sears me from the inside.

God, he's just so *big*.

Wait, did I say that out loud?

"You like it," he grunts in response, shifting his weight to one arm so his other can hitch my knee up higher, opening me. "This cunt needs to be stuffed full, doesn't it? Goddamn it, Savvy, you feel so fucking good."

I don't think he's ever said my actual name when he's inside me, and it makes my heart beat faster. "Dar," I moan, dragging him down to kiss me, even as the deep, rough way he fucks me becomes too much and reduces me to a writhing mess beneath him.

So suddenly that it makes me dizzy, he rolls us, and I find myself sitting astride him, his cock still buried deep.

I don't hesitate. Planting my hands on the center of his chest, I roll my hips, finding an angle that grinds my clit on the base of his cock.

"That's it. Ride me," Dar commands, and the way he's looking at me… I'm positive I've never felt so beautiful, so desired. There's not a single worry that he doesn't like the color of my nipples, or wishes my breasts were bigger or my ass was smaller. Not when the opposite is written all over his face.

I love him.

I love him.

I really, really love him.

It's on the tip of my tongue, so close to bursting out, but a tiny fissure of fear catches the words in my throat. I dive forward instead, slanting my lips over his in an urgent kiss. I'm so close, vibrating on the edge, and the sharp jolt of pain mixed with pleasure as Dar's fingers find my piercings is all it takes to send me over.

I come, my hoarse cry muffled by his kiss, my orgasm extended on and on by the cock driving into me from below.

"There you go." A hand comes down on my ass, hard enough to make me squeal, and I take the hint. Dar's eyes flash as he watches me sit back, his hands digging into my hips to guide my pace. "I could watch you do this all night," he groans, even as his jaw strains. I double my efforts, determined to make him come.

I let out a breathy laugh. "You can take a video if you want."

Another spank. "I canceled a very important meeting because I needed to get back here and fuck you again. Are you pleased with yourself?"

"Kind of, yeah."

The smack sounds louder this time, and my rhythm stutters as he hits the same tender spot he spanked before. "Be a good girl for me, baby. Make me come."

His words make need twist in my belly and, holding his gaze, I lift my fingers to my breasts, teasing and pinching myself as I ride him faster. Dar's hands grip my hips, his quiet noises of praise and pleasure making me even more determined, more desperate, to make this as incredible for him as it is for me.

How is it even possible to be this attracted to someone?

"I want it inside me," I whine, my thighs sticking to his sides. "Come in me, Dar, please."

With a low curse, his hands drag me down, sealing us together as his length swells and twitches. I fall forward, and the feeling of wet heat blooming in the deepest part of me makes me come too, trembling with my forehead pressed to his chest.

Even as our heartbeats calm and the sweat cools on our skin, we keep holding each other.

Finally, Dar presses a kiss to the top of my head and pulls out, shifting us over so we lay side by side on my pillow. "Hi," he says quietly, his eyes searching my face.

My cheeks ache with how big my answering smile is. "Hi," I whisper, so full of feelings for this man that it seems like a miracle they're not coming out of my nose.

Every time I think I can't possibly fall any harder, I'm proven wrong. Shouldn't there be a limit to how much space a single person takes up in your heart? A maximum capacity? *Sorry, only one piece of my soul per customer?*

Apparently not.

Reaching down to retrieve the jumble of crumpled bedding at the end of the mattress, I pull it over both of us and burrow closer into his warm, hard, Dar-smelling chest.

The lights are still on, but neither of us move to turn them off as our breathing grows slow and measured.

Fingers skim lazily over the words inked on my ribs, *his* words. "Hey, Dar?"

He hums, already falling asleep.

"You're going to fix the window in the morning."

To Do: ⭐

- ~~Find a realtor for GG~~
- ~~Meeting with accountant~~
- Find an accountant
- Exact revenge on Caleb
- ~~Clean literally everything~~
- Fix literally everything
- ~~Talk to HIM~~
- ~~New Vacuum~~
- ~~Rip up stained carpet in lobby+snackbar~~
- ~~Replace those long lightbulbs in the ceiling~~
- Find out which games in arcade don't work
- ~~Fix roof leak~~
- ~~Reconnect security system (at some point)~~
- Find a therapist
- ~~Figure out why my car is making that clanky noise~~
- ~~New bathroom light fixture~~
- ~~Research competitor pricing~~
- ~~Complete the Google Ads course~~
- ~~Locate source of weird smell in back hallway~~
- ~~Buy tampons!!!!!!!!~~
- ~~Finish new website~~
- ~~Create social media graphics for Laser Speed Dating~~
- ~~Start ads on b-day parties~~
- Get a ~~bikini wax~~ like now
- ~~Train kids on new POS system~~

- ~~Kids paint B-day rooms~~
- Stock arcade games
- Stock snack bar
- ~~Update business hours~~
- New business bank account (Me +Dar only registered users)
- Paint wheel purple+green
- Job posting!

CHAPTER 19
DARWIN

SAVVY HAS BEEN SLEEPING in my bed for a week now.

Not coincidentally, it's also been the happiest week of my life.

I don't deserve her, not even close, but I'm sure as hell trying to. What I said to Raven the day she and her family came to help us clean was the truth: Savvy wants me, and I'd be a fool not to take that and run like hell.

"You should move in." The words slip out before I can stop them, but I'm hardly responsible for my lack of self-control.

When I came into the kitchen a moment ago, I found my girlfriend standing at the stove, barefoot and dressed only in one of my T-shirts, pink hair gathered on top of her head in a messy bun.

The room is more cluttered than it used to be. There are onions in the fruit bowl and oat milk in the fridge. At the table, my laptop is sitting across from Savvy's in the spots where we've taken to working after dinner every night. There's also a sticky note with a very accurate drawing of my cock (with an arrow pointing to it, accompanied by the words

Darwin's Dick so there's no mistaking it) stuck to the pantry door.

Everywhere I look, there are signs of my little tornado making herself at home. As I come up behind her, wrapping my arms around her warm waist and feeling the comfort—the fucking *comfort*—of having her close... The words just come out.

And Savvy goes stiff.

It's only for half a second, then she's back to pushing eggs around the pan with a spatula. Her voice is casual as she responds, "It's a little soon, don't you think?"

I wish I could see her face right now. Frowning, I lean in to kiss her jaw. "No. I don't," I mumble into her skin, attempting to ignore the panic crawling up my spine. "If you're not ready, though, I understand."

Savvy turns off the burner and begins transferring the eggs onto the two plates she has waiting with toast and sliced melon. "It's not that I'm not ready," she admits, offering me a gentle, reassuring smile as she hands me my breakfast.

I kiss her in thanks, and we move over to the table. "What is it, then?" I ask as we sit. The familiar, anxious tightening is going on in my chest, and I know I need to get my head on straight, but hearing her response seems so much more important right now.

Rolling her fork between her fingers, Savvy gazes at me apprehensively. "Please don't take this personally. It's just that I might not... love this house."

"You don't love the house?" I echo, looking around the familiar space and trying to imagine it through Savvy's eyes. It's bigger and nicer than Stone's place, and in a better area of town. There's a lot of white, admittedly, but that isn't difficult to change. "We could... paint?" I suggest, looking back at her quizzically.

Her nose wrinkles as she swallows a bite of melon. "*Um,* maybe."

Even without that lackluster response, I would still know she isn't a fan of this plan. Below the tabletop, my knee bounces. I need to take a step back, clear my head and do the breathing exercises I learned from Doctor Lucas, but I'm too anxious to think straight.

Sensing I'm not buying this, Savvy sighs, setting down her fork. "I'm not saying no. It's just something I'd need to wrap my head around. We'll keep talking about it."

"You shouldn't have to live somewhere you don't like."

"Dar," she pleads, eyes wide and imploring. "I'm trying to be honest with you."

I grit my teeth. "So tell me what's wrong with the damn house!" Savvy's face falls, and my stomach lurches with regret. I lower my voice. "I'm sorry. This is… I'm on edge. I'm sorry."

She nods, her hands slipping off the table and into her lap. "It's okay. I'm not communicating well."

"It's not an excuse for me to raise my voice."

We stare at each other in silence for a long moment. Finally, Savvy sighs again. "This place just brings up a lot of sad memories for me. I'm happy now, and I know you are too, but there's a lot of not-so-great history here. For *both of us.*"

There's a painful lump in my throat that won't seem to dislodge. "I didn't realize you felt that way."

Her lips lift in a halfhearted smile, eyes pleading with me to understand. "It's your home. You love this house, and I… I want to be with you. We don't need to talk about this now. It's a down-the-road conversation."

I love *her*, not the fucking house.

I want to tell her we'll put it on the market and find something new together. In fact, imagining myself walking hand in hand with Savvy through houses, discussing square footage and bathroom tile… I love it.

But she isn't asking me for that. If she hates this house but isn't suggesting we find a new one, could it be because she doesn't see *us* as permanent?

Ice is seeping through my veins, and beneath the table, my leg bounces faster.

For fuck's sake, she told me on that very first day here she wanted to sell the business. That's what we've been working toward. How did I manage to ignore that? Have I spent the last months helping her leave me?

Galactic Guild is done, and looks better than I've ever seen it. There are only a few days until our soft opening, and Savvy has already sold out birthday party packages and Laser Speed Dating events for the next two months. We worked out a financial projection spreadsheet last weekend, and it had us comfortably in the green within three months. We could get an offer any day now.

My chest feels like it's going to cave in, and when Savvy reaches across the table to take my hand, I rip it back. Her face falls.

"Dar," she begins cautiously, "can you tell me what you're thinking right now?"

The prickle of irritation I feel is almost a relief. "Not everything is my OCD, Savvy."

"I didn't say it was!"

"You thought it," I snarl, shoving my chair back and pacing to the sink to fill a glass of water. As the faucet turns on, though, I push my hands under the stream instead. My muscles are working of their own volition, moving through the familiar ritual before I even realize what I'm doing.

Some of my tension bleeds away.

Savvy is still sitting at the table, and I don't want to look at her. I don't want to see her hurt or anger and know that I'm entirely at fault for it. She hasn't done anything. This entire conversation, and the ugly turn it's taken, is on me.

I'm not equipped for this. Feelings. People. *Love.*

Savvy doesn't like this house? Well, this house is the only

place I've ever been comfortable, and I won't leave it for someone who could walk away on a whim. Then what would I be left with? One by one, the ties holding me to my old life have been cut and this one, the house, is the largest. I can't let it go. I just can't.

"Please stop washing your hands."

I start. She's standing across the kitchen island from me now, and her voice trembles. Looking down, I see there's soap on my hands. I don't remember putting soap… Gritting my teeth, I rinse the suds, then turn the faucet off and lean forward, bracing my hands on the counter.

It's a struggle to gather enough courage to look up at her, but I do, steeling myself for what I'm about to see.

Savvy has her arms wrapped around herself, and my heart wrenches when I see the worry in her eyes. *Worry.* Not anger or hurt, despite me being a world-class prick.

Her voice is unbearably understanding. "Do you need some space?"

No, I don't need space. I need to be good enough for this woman, good enough to be *good for her*, and I don't know how. Could I?

How the hell did we get here?

Last night after work, we went out to dinner. At a restaurant. It was a busy night in town, and we sat at a cramped table in a line of other couples, making easy conversation over drinks and sharing an appetizer. I made her laugh.

An hour ago, I woke to her mouth lavishing attention on my hard cock, bright eyes glinting mischievously up at me in the early morning light. I'd let her play until I was close, then rolled her onto her back, finding my way into her body so easily it's like we'd done this a thousand times before.

For weeks, I've been letting myself believe I'm normal, feeling triumphant over a few insignificant victories. Now, the illusion is crumbling down around me, and the woman I love looks like I'm breaking her heart.

I can't fucking breathe.

"Are you going to sell Galactic Guild?"

Savvy's eyes widen. "What? I don't... I'm not sure. What does this have to do with the house?"

The house? Christ, that's what we were talking about, wasn't it? Her not liking this house isn't the issue anymore, but how could she know that? I haven't been talking to her as this mental spiral takes me miles away from our original fight.

I scrub my hands over my face. This is terrible. More than anything, I want to apologize, to move forward and bury this shitty morning under a thousand incredible ones. Even for a man who has never fallen in love before, I know this thing between us is special. *She* is special, and the single best thing that's ever happened to me.

Could I make her happy, though? Am I capable of that? Or will I have saddled her with an old man with a malfunctioning brain?

I have to think, and I can't do it when the love of my life is staring at me with tears in her eyes, because right now, my only priority is making her smile again.

Sucking in one last lungful of air, I let my hands fall. "Space would be good." My voice sounds cold, detached even, and Savvy curls further in on herself.

She nods, valiantly trying to pretend I haven't hurt her. Despite offering, I can tell she didn't expect me to agree. "Okay. I'll just... I'll get my stuff and get ready for work at home."

Every instinct she awoke inside me is howling with protest, but I can't move as she walks back to the table, unplugging her computer and gathering it up without looking at me.

The breakfast she made us is still untouched on the table. I open my mouth to tell her to stay and eat with me, or that I'll go and she can wait here. Nothing comes out. Then, her bare footsteps are retreating toward the bedroom, and still I'm frozen to the spot.

Seconds tick by, or maybe minutes, and I stare into the sink, trying to recreate the events that led us here as panic and self-disgust mount higher inside me.

I only look up when Savvy reemerges, dressed with an overstuffed tote bag over her shoulder. Her eyes are rimmed with red.

"Okay," she says, her tone determinately calm, scanning the kitchen to make sure there isn't anything she missed. Finally, when she can't put it off any longer, she lifts her gaze to meet mine. "Dar, if the house is a deal breaker, we'll work it out, okay? I'm sorry I said no like that. I'd... I'd live anywhere as long as it's with you."

I clutch the countertop as she turns away, hurrying out of sight. As soon as the front door closes behind her, I'm struck by a horrible sense of *déjà vu.*

An eighteen-year-old Savvy, running into the rain with tears streaming down her face.

Savvy on the day she came back into my life, fleeing as quickly as she could.

Is it any wonder she doesn't love this place? For god's sake, this room alone bore witness to the lowest point in our relationship. There's not enough paint in the world to cover that up.

Am I so terrified of losing of my comfort zone that I would ask Savvy, *my little tornado,* to live in the place where I broke her heart? How could I be so fucking selfish? How could I allow my fear to spiral so far that I begin to question her place in my life, when all she's done is prove the opposite?

It's a miracle I don't crumple under the weight of my regret and self- loathing.

She didn't do anything wrong. Savvy was acting like an adult. She communicated her feelings and compromised with mine because—as desperately as I'm trying not to think about it at the moment—I *know* she loves me. We've never exchanged those words, but every minute I'm with her, I feel it.

Savvy sees past the disorder that's dominated my entire life thus far. She sees *me*, and in return, I let her leave this house in tears.

As my eyes fall to the abandoned breakfast plates, my stomach churns violently.

I think I'm going to be sick.

CHAPTER 20
SAVVY

'M TRYING NOT to panic.

The entire drive home, my hand keeps drifting to the little switch on the side of my phone that controls the ringer volume, checking that it's on. I keep expecting to find that it's turned itself off or I somehow mixed up the correct position, as if the piece of metal is responsible for Dar not immediately calling me to come back.

It's not reasonable to expect him to. I offered him space, and he took it.

That doesn't mean… We had a fight, that's all. Couples fight. It's normal.

That's what I keep telling myself, anyway, trying to reason away the icy ball of dread that has settled in the pit of my stomach. The one that gets heavier and heavier every time I touch that stupid switch.

Dar is going to call and tell me to turn around. He needed a minute to breathe, but he'll call. *He has to call.*

This is supposed to be different than every other shitty relationship I've had, the ones I thought were special or important but now pale in comparison to the feelings I have for Dar. I'm in love with him, like, *completely* in love with him.

The kind of love that doesn't get thrown off track by stupid arguments or misunderstandings. The kind of love that's *forever*, damn it.

What if, with one stupid comment, I made him realize that this—*us*—is more trouble than it's worth? He's already had to change so much just to allow me a place in his life, and while I thought he was happy to do it, what if I was wrong all along?

Then, on top of the hurt, I keep thinking about the way his hands moved under the water at the kitchen sink and how he reached for the soap like a lifeline. Stress and big life changes aggravate OCD; I'm not an expert, but I know that much. My suggesting that he would have to leave the place where he's most comfortable to have me in his life full time was the emotional equivalent of setting the kitchen on fire.

As I turn into the driveway of Dad's house and shift the car into park, the last sliver of hope that this will quickly be over dies. My eyes burn with unshed tears, and, for a moment, all I can do is stare at the cracked garage door pane, trying to make sense of the last half hour.

Was it really just thirty minutes? It seems impossible that I could have felt perfectly happy such a short time ago when I now feel like my whole world is crumbling around me.

Hollowed out and endeavoring not to cry in front of the sour Mrs. Paul while she prunes her rose bushes, I push the car door open and step out onto the drive, wiping my eyes.

There's no comfort in coming back here, to my supposed home. Even with my name on the deed and most of my stuff in boxes in the garage, it still feels so much more like Dad's house than mine. He's been gone for over two months now, and I haven't gotten around to clearing out his bedroom or listing his hundreds of collectibles on eBay.

I've just made it to the walkway that leads to the front door when the sound of a car turning quickly into the cul-de-sac makes me glance back toward the road. From here, there's a clear view of the entire street, including a familiar car speeding toward me.

My heart stalls.

I watch, filled with reluctant, terrified hope, as the driver turns sharply into my driveway, almost upsetting the big rolling trash can at the curb. A ragged little sob bubbles from my lips as the car stops and my eyes meet Dar's through the windshield.

Seconds later, he's on his feet, not even bothering to shut the car door as he closes the distance between us in long strides. Without a single word, he wraps his arms around me, pulling me into his chest so forcefully that he sweeps me off the ground.

He's shaking.

"I'm sorry." Two raw, pleading words, and *I know* we're going to be okay. "I'm sorry, baby. I'm so fucking sorry."

Wrapping my legs around his waist, I press my forehead to his, making sure he can see my eyes. "I know. I know, Dar. It's okay—"

"It's not," he interrupts, his voice weak. "It's not okay, Savvy. Fuck, I never want to make you feel that way again. Never. We'll sell the house. Stone's too, if you want, and buy a new place together. Or I can move in here. I don't care."

"Dar, it's your safe space. We can—" I begin, but he's already shaking his head.

"No. No, Savvy. *You* are my safe space. *You* are my home —*you* are my fucking *partner*." His voice cracks, and his arms tighten around me as tears spill over my cheeks. "Baby, I love you. I'm so in love with you. It's impossible for me to stop feeling guilty for the impact my disorder will have on your life. You deserve perfection, and I'm the furthest thing from that. I trust you, though, more than I've ever trusted anyone. If you tell me you're in this, that you can handle it, then we'll figure out the rest."

I'm nodding before he's finished speaking. I've never felt

this way before, have never experienced so much relief and fear and hope all at once.

Life is messy. Fights and misunderstandings happen. Dar's disorder will never stop being something we need to watch, and I'm hardly without my own issues.

Things won't be perfect. I don't want them to be.

I want someone who is going to screw up, then break speed limits to come after me and fix it because he loves me as much as I love him.

Still wrapped around Dar like a monkey, standing on my father's walkway with the disapproving eyes of Mrs. Paul from next door on us, my hands frame his face. "I'm in this."

His throat bobs, worry still shining in his dark eyes even while holding me tighter. "Just like that?"

"Yup." My smile is effortless as the last shadows of fear and doubt fall, replaced by so much happiness that it might last me forever. "I love you too, Wilder. Got a problem with that?"

The hot, demanding kiss I get in response confirms he does not, in fact, have a problem with that.

We sway on the spot, clinging to each other, until Dar has the presence of mind to begin moving toward the front door. "Say it again," he rasps, and I can tell by the tremor in his muscles that he isn't quite past the fear and guilt that prompted him to follow me here.

I work my fingers through the coarse hairs of his beard, loving the way he leans into my touch, like he craves it. It's not something I'll ever take for granted. "I love you."

Another searing kiss, but we break apart laughing when he steps off the walkway and has to pause to yank his leg out of a bush.

"You can put me down," I pant as we resume our path, Dar's hands palming my ass.

He shakes his head, reaching blindly into the bag still

hanging over my shoulder in search of my keys. "I'm… I'm not okay right now, Savvy. I need you close."

"I love you," I promise again, and my back hits the front door, pinned in place as our lips meet once more. His teeth graze my bottom lip, and the tiny gesture makes me melt, arching closer.

"Fuck, baby," he groans, pulling away to fumble one-handed with my keys. I attack his neck, kissing and biting as wetness coats my panties. The friction I'm getting from rocking against him isn't enough.

There are things we need to talk about and I have to get to work soon, but even if I were physically capable of peeling myself off this man (which I'm not), I wouldn't do it. Ten minutes ago, I was fighting back tears, not sure what the future held, and now Dar is holding me in his arms and promising to love me forever.

Responsibility can suck it.

Clattering through the door, Dar only narrowly avoids tripping over the bunched-up entryway mat, but he still doesn't release me. Urgency is strung tightly between us, pulling with every step. By the time we make it into the living room, both of us are panting.

"I need you." I don't want to let go of him, but there doesn't seem to be a way around it.

As my feet find the floor and my hands move to the hem of my T-shirt, though, Dar stops me. "Let me."

Oh god.

He undresses me with a level of self-restraint that's torturous. The silence in the house presses in on us, making every gasp or rustle of clothing so much more erotic. When the last piece falls to the ground, so does Dar. He kneels at my feet, dropping hot, wet kisses from my belly button up to each pebbled nipple, taking his time laving attention on both.

"Dar," I plead, gripping his shoulders as he moves to my ribs, skimming his nose over the dark ink there.

There's a quiet grunt in response. "I'm going to marry you someday."

My heart shoots into my throat. "Okay."

"Properly," he continues, kissing each word of my tattoo. "You'll wear a dress. There will be people there. We're going to dance."

Tears are burning behind my eyes, the raw emotion of the moment bleeding into the frustration and need that's still so potent. "I'd like that," I whisper, barely able to speak past the heart still lodged in my throat.

His hands start at the backs of my ankles and move upward, touching every inch of me, except where I need him most. They pause on my lower back, and Dar lifts his gaze to mine.

How could I ever have thought his eyes are cold? There's so much there. Love and hope and joy. My whole future, staring back at me.

"I'm going to build us a home."

I nod, my bottom lip trembling. "I'd like that too."

His smile is breathtaking. "I'm going to get you pregnant."

My answering laugh is bordering on hysterical. "We can start practicing now, if you want."

He does want.

I giggle as I collapse back onto the floor, my thighs spread. Dar is still dressed in the sweatpants and T-shirt he was wearing earlier, and my mouth goes dry when I see the little dark spot over the head of his cock. A second later, it's gone, and Dar is hovering over me, naked and hungry.

He doesn't check if I'm ready for him; we both know I am. And when he fists his cock, guiding all those inches into my body, my back bows off the floor and a cry shatters the quiet of the house.

"*Shhh.*" My back burns as his first thrust pushes me over the carpet. Dar grunts in pleasure, pressing his forehead to mine, and the noise alone is enough to make me wetter. "You're mine now, baby. No going back."

Another powerful thrust, and I can sense he's losing it.

I love the change that comes over him when he's inside me. It's gradual at first, his control slipping with every smooth pump of his hips, until he can't help but lose himself in me, his body taking what it needs from mine.

Nothing turns me on more.

"Yours," I echo, and his pace begins to stutter. "You can do what you like with me."

Dar curses, and the arms framing my body flex. "Yeah? Hold your legs open—*yeah*, like that—gonna fuck you rough now."

My hands grip the backs of my knees, holding myself open and exposed as the man on top of me lets loose.

Every muscle in his body is strained as he pulls back and drives forward, bearing down on me with all his strength and fucking me into the carpet. Our lips meet, and he kisses me, muffling my cries.

I thought I'd seen Dar unleashed before, but it wasn't like this. We're both flayed open, raw and vulnerable from the events of this morning, and it's like he's trying to get deeper than he ever has.

"So goddamn tight, every fucking time, baby," he groans against my lips, one hand winding through my hair and pulling hard enough for it to hurt.

I'm shaking now, and the wet slap of his cock is getting faster. We've barely begun, and already I feel my orgasm threatening to swallow me whole.

He knows it too.

The hand in my hair tightens. "Watch," Dar grits out. "Watch me fuck you."

He lifts himself off me, just enough for me to look between our bodies, and my mouth falls open at what I see. It's *primal*. He's big and hard, and I'm small and soft, but the differences between us don't stop him from needing me. He pumps and pumps, takes and takes, and I don't realize that he's giving too until my orgasm swallows me whole.

I come, clawing at his back as lights burst inside my eyelids and my breaths come in ragged sobs. Dar isn't far behind. I've barely begun to collapse back onto the carpet when he presses deep, his face slack with pleasure as his cum fills me.

It's *everything*.

"Oh my god," I half laugh, half cry, my muscles weak as the man I love showers my face with kisses, his big hands cradling my face. The sweetness of the moment should be strange after the roughness of our coupling, but it's not.

Dar collapses onto his back beside me, reaching up to wipe damp hair off his forehead.

We gaze at each other.

"I really am going to do it," he says quietly, his hand finding mine in the space between us.

My heart flutters. "Which one? Marry me? Get me pregnant? Build us a house?"

"Yes." His tone is so dry and matter-of-fact that I laugh, rolling over to press my face into his neck and breathe in his familiar warm, morning smell. "I'm not going to sell Galactic Guild." I hadn't decided until this moment, but as soon as I say the words out loud, I know they're right.

Dar hums, kissing the crown of my hair. "Don't keep it because you think I want you to. I was scared, Savvy. I thought… I don't know what I thought, but it wasn't the truth."

"It was the OCD talking?"

He nods jerkily, and I curl closer, holding him tighter. "I love you so much. It fucking kills me that this has become your problem too."

"If it were me, would you think it's too much to handle?"

"*Of course not.*" He sounds offended that I even asked.

I flick him. "Well then. We're in this together. *Partners,* remember? Maybe we should schedule some sessions with your therapist so I can stop consulting Doctor Google about the best ways to support you."

Dar blows out a shaky breath, and I feel him nod. "Yes. That's—yes."

Kissing his chest one more time, I sit up, stretching. "And I'm not keeping Galactic Guild because you want me to."

"Why, then?" he asks, following me into a seated position and reaching for his pants.

I hesitate. "It's kind of... proof that I'm more than I thought I was. Before this, I think I got comfortable with being a failure. Losing jobs, sabotaging relationships, letting my college roommate pierce my nipples—"

"*That's* where you got them?"

"Yup. I almost had to take them out because of the infections, but I got some antibiotics at the tropical fish store and it cleared right up." There's a choking noise to my right, and I grin, reaching for my panties. "Anyway, I just kind of accepted I was an idiot, but when I had no other option than to succeed, I did it. I mean, maybe. We haven't even opened yet. Things are going in the right direction, at least."

I start to get to my feet, but a warm hand catches my hand. I turn to look at Dar, who is gazing at me wearing my favorite stern-principal expression. "You did it, Savvy."

My heart is so full as I nod. "Yeah. I guess I did."

To Do: ⭐

~~Find a realtor for GG~~   ~~Kids paint B-day rooms~~

~~Meeting with accountant~~   ~~Stock arcade games~~

Find an accountant   ~~Stock snack bar~~

Exact revenge on Caleb   ~~Update business hours~~

~~Clean literally everything~~   ~~New business bank account (Me~~

~~Fix literally everything~~   ~~+Dar only registered users)~~

~~Talk to HIM~~   ~~Paint wheel purple-green~~

~~New Vacuum~~   ~~Job posting!~~

~~Rip up stained carpet in lobby+snackbar~~

~~Replace those long lightbulbs in the ceiling~~

Find out which games in arcade don't work

~~Fix roof leak~~

~~Reconnect security system (at some point)~~

~~Find a therapist~~ First appointment 7/8 @ 2:30

~~Figure out why my car is making that clanky noise~~

~~New bathroom light fixture~~

~~Research competitor pricing~~

~~Complete the Google Ads course~~

~~Locate source of weird smell in back hallway~~

~~Buy tampons!!!!!!!!~~

~~Finish new website~~

~~Create social media graphics for Laser Speed Dating~~

~~Start ads on b-day parties~~

Get a ~~bikini wax~~ like now

~~Train kids on new POS system~~

CHAPTER 21
DARWIN

'M NOT EQUIPPED to lie to Savvy.

Even if it's for a good reason and I'm confident she'll be happy I did, I've been on edge all morning.

"Opening day!" she chirps around the toothbrush in her mouth—so it actually sounds more like "openy-ay"—beaming at me in the mirror.

I love seeing her like this: barefaced and happy, dressed in another of my stolen T-shirts while standing at the second sink in my bathroom, the one that was never used until she started staying over. Her hair is damp from the shower we took together, and the bathroom smells like her shampoo and my body wash. Today, however, I'm too distracted to appreciate the warm, casual domesticity as much as I normally do.

Spitting out my own toothpaste, I rinse my mouth and lean over to kiss her temple. "I told the kids they could start at nine. Will you be ready to go in five?"

I know she won't be. Previous experience has taught me she needs at least thirty minutes to get ready to go anywhere, longer if she recently showered. Sure enough, Savvy's eyes widen at the question, and she leans over to spit.

"You're telling me this *now*?" she groans, gesturing to herself. "I still have wet hair, Dar."

"I'm sorry. Slipped my mind."

She sighs heavily. "We'll have to take separate cars. They really don't need to be in a full hour early. This is just the soft opening, so I'm guessing only a handful of people will show. Don't let Luke work the snack bar, okay? He never stops sneaking pepperoni. Put King on there. Oh! And remind Marley about that breaker in the arena, just in case it pops during a game—"

"I've got it, baby." I nudge her chin up, grinning as I see her annoyance with me melt away. "It's going to go great. You've thought of everything. And if you haven't, that's the point of having a soft opening, right? To find out what the issues are before you guys start regular business hours? You have those interviews set up next week too, so you'll have plenty of staff."

Biting her lip, she nods, accepting the truth in this. "I know."

"I'll see you there."

Another kiss, and I've turned on my heel, heart racing as if I've just committed a robbery. Christ, I have no idea how people keep things from their partners. This entire plan has been an anxiety-inducing nightmare. Savvy will be lucky if I keep her birthday gifts a secret after this.

Even after I've successfully escaped the house without my girlfriend realizing anything is amiss, the nerves don't subside. I want to do this, damn it. For Savvy, and for myself. It's important to me, but that doesn't make it any easier.

I even considered calling the whole thing off a few times, but the fight two days ago strengthened my resolve.

Savvy deserves a grand gesture. That's how it's done in the books and the movies, and virtually every romantic piece of subculture that's ever been shoved under my nose, isn't it?

When you screw up and hurt the person you love, saying you're sorry isn't enough sometimes.

I'm certain she's put the whole thing behind her and is happy to love me unconditionally until the end of time with no further apologies. But, in five years, or ten, or twenty, when my little tornado looks at me, I don't want there to be a doubt in her mind that I would move mountains for her.

That starts right fucking now.

Even with all that, however, I'm still anxious as I turn onto the road leading to Galactic Guild. Especially when I see the cars parked along either side of the road for easily a quarter of a mile before the parking lot.

My fingers drum restlessly on the steering wheel as I experience the familiar restless, crawling sensation beneath my skin. I haven't done anything like this in over a decade, since just after my second book was released. Despite my agent's misgivings, I realized my publisher wanted more books out of me far more than they wanted someone to sit behind signing tables and show up to conventions, so I started refusing all of it.

I gave the odd interview, sure, but the rise of my success correlated with the worsening of my symptoms, and I engaged with readers less and less. Now, with a new series beginning to take shape, I need to do better. One event won't change that, but it's an attempt, *a start*, and the fact it will benefit Savvy too?

I'm going to do this.

When I reach the parking lot, it's apparent why there are cars lining the road. The parking lot is completely packed, with a line of people stretching around the entire building and out of sight beyond a line of parked cars. All of them are clutching books. Some near the front have folding chairs and are sharing bags of chips.

Christ, all this is for *me*?

I feel like I can breathe again as I drive around to park

beside the dumpsters. Thankfully, there's no one back here. As I step out of the car, though, a metal door along the back of the building opens, and Marley pops her head out.

"Did you see that line?" she gushes, practically bouncing as she steps out of the way to let me into the back hall.

"Yeah, I saw it," I confirm gravely, rolling up the sleeves of my dress shirt as I follow her toward the lobby. A strange sense of calm has settled on me, and it's almost more unnerving than outright panic.

This should be harder, shouldn't it?

Marley flicks her hair over her shoulder. "I told a bunch of the guys at the game shop that I got to help you with this, and they didn't believe me. Sexist dickwads. Anyway, they've been sitting outside in the heat for four hours, but I'd really like to *see* the karmic justice taking place. So, I was thinking I'd give you a signal when they get to your table, and you could write 'Marley is your queen' in their books."

"I'm not doing that," I tell her flatly, just as we emerge into the lobby.

The windows have been tinted, but I can still hear the rumble of excited voices and see the vague shadows of people moving around. There's no time to lose my shit, though, because a tall, dark-haired young woman is walking toward me. Scowling.

"I wasn't sure you'd come."

Raven sniffs, crossing her arms. "I'm helping for Savvy. Not you."

I let out a hard laugh. "I figured. Thank you nonetheless."

She stares at me for a moment. "So, you're serious about this? Her? You're not just looking to have your ego stroked?"

Lifting a hand to our current surroundings, I smile tightly. "If you've Googled me, even once, you'll know that this isn't a thing I do. I think it's fairly obvious my ego isn't a priority."

Raven doesn't argue with this, but her expression is

pinched. "You must think I'm a bitch for icing her out after I found out she was seeing you."

I hesitate. "I think you've been there for her for a long time, and it's difficult to see someone you care about do something that's bad for them. Given our history, I can't exactly blame you for being angry."

Raven nods, stepping back. "Okay, then. Don't think this means I approve of you."

"I wouldn't dare."

"You're on probation, for probably the rest of your life. Which might be shorter than you think, by the way. Savvy sometimes forgets to turn off the burners when she finishes cooking."

Noted.

Raven retreats, off on her mission to retrieve Savvy, and I feel lighter. My agent managed to assemble a last-minute team to manage the event and set up the birthday party room for the signing, but Raven, her boyfriend, Luke, Marley, and King will be the only ones on hand to make sure that Galactic Guild doesn't crumple under the weight of hundreds of new customers.

It's one hell of a trial run. For me, and the business.

One of the event staff approach. "We're ready for you, Mr. Wilder."

———

Savvy arrives about forty-five minutes after we've started.

She slips into the room, face pale, and watches from the doorway as I finish signing a complete set of my books for a trio of readers, who are excitedly telling me their thoughts on the casting for the show. I meet her eyes over their heads and feel myself grin.

As soon as I've thanked them for coming and they've headed out, I hold up a hand to stop my PA from sending in the next group, and Savvy walks around the back of the table.

"What did you do?" She laughs, a little hysterically. "The arena is booked for games all week, the arcade is packed, and there is *a line around the building* to get in here. There isn't a single birthday party spot open for the next six months."

I turn, pulling her to stand in the space between my legs. "Are you happy?"

"I mean, yeah, but—" Another mad giggle, and she shakes her head. "I can't believe this, Dar. We'll have to open another location at this rate."

"*You* will," I correct. "I'll always be here to support you, but this is your thing, Savvy. You brought this place back from the dead, and I'll sit here signing books all month if that's what it takes for it to get the attention it deserves."

At this point, her knees seem to give out. I pull her onto my lap, kissing her gently.

"I love you," she whispers, shaking her head. "I can't wrap my head around this. You didn't have to do this for me."

I swallow the lump in my throat. "It's not just for you. It's for me, and… it's for Stone too."

She stills, and I know why. We haven't discussed her father, not since she asked me for help with his ashes. Neither of us have broached the subject of how he would feel about our relationship.

Savvy blows out a long, shaky breath. "I think he would have been proud of me."

"He *absolutely* would have been. He was flawed, but he loved you, and he loved this place. Seeing you take something so important to him and make it better than he ever could? Nothing would have made Stone prouder."

Savvy wipes her eyes, sniffing. "We should talk about this some other time so you don't have to sign books while holding your sobbing partner in your arms."

"I would do that."

"I know you would, but I should try to maintain some dignity in front of future customers." She laughs, kissing me again before getting to her feet. "You're the sweetest grump in the world, Darwin Wilder, and I love you."

Before she moves away, though, I catch her hand in mine. "I have one more surprise for you."

Savvy's eyebrows knit together when I nod to a large cardboard box in the corner. My heart lodges in my throat as she crosses to it and opens the top, staring down in confusion at the metallic contents.

"Take it out," I encourage gently, and she does.

It's a trophy. The base is a rough stone, giving way to a laser tag gun that's pointed skyward. On the base, engraved on a black plaque, are the words "The Stone Cup".

Savvy's expression is unreadable as she looks over at me. "Is this…"

I nod. "I found a metal-work company that specializes in memorial pieces. When you mentioned continuing the annual laser tag tournament, I thought it would be appropriate. There's a carpenter coming next week to build a special case for it behind the desk."

She isn't saying anything, though, and for the first time since I had the idea, I feel a flicker of apprehension. Still, I stay quiet, watching as Savvy bends to settle the trophy back inside its box. When she turns back to look at me, her eyes are shining. "It's perfect."

Emotion tightens in my chest. "Yeah?"

She nods. "Yeah."

It's another five minutes before I'm ready to resume the signing, but my little tornado stays close. She offers to take over for my PA, darting in and out of the room for the next hour, bringing in books and chatting happily with people in line.

"Wow, you've got the coolest boss ever, huh?" asks a guy

in one group, and before Savvy has even opened her mouth, I've corrected him.

"She's my partner, actually." I smile, shaking out my aching right hand as I open his book. "Would you like it made out to you?"

He nods eagerly. "Yeah, thanks. I'm Caleb. This is so cool, you're my favorite author. I can't believe you're from around here."

I write out his name and sign mine, but before I can slide the book back to him, Savvy's hand slaps down on top of it, stopping me. She glowers over the table at the man.

"Have you ever been here before, *Caleb*?"

He blinks at her and grins nervously, obviously taken aback by the animosity. "Uh, yeah? A few times. I live close by."

Bemused, I look between them. "Uh—"

Savvy holds up a finger to silence me, her eyes narrowed. "When's the last time you stopped by?"

The guy swallows, glancing at me then back to Savvy. "A few months ago, maybe? I can't remember."

"Ever use the bathroom?"

"What?" His face has gone bright pink, and his friends are exchanging curious looks behind his back. "I, I think so? Probably?" An uncomfortable laugh follows this pronouncement, and Savvy's lip curls.

I've never seen her look so murderous.

"You think so, huh? Create anything special in there?"

Caleb gapes at Savvy like a fish, opening and closing his mouth.

Without another word, my little tornado pulls the book out from under my hand, opens it, and rips out the title page I just signed. As Caleb and I watch, she takes the bright-blue pen held loosely in my hand and scrawls something below the copyright information. I lean over to see.

Caleb's Caca Lies Here.

Beaming, she shoves it back at him. "Thanks for stopping by, *Caleb*. You might want to consider adding some fiber to your diet."

Face now alarmingly red, Caleb's eyes flick to me, clearly hoping for support. When he receives none, he takes his book and backs away. Savvy's leer doesn't falter until he and his friends have left.

"Are you going to tell me what that was about?" I ask her mildly as I offer the next group filing in a polite smile.

"Oh, nothing important." She sighs happily, bending to kiss my cheek. "The universe is just so awesome sometimes, don't you think?"

I watch her walk off, pink ponytail bouncing, and adoration swells inside me.

"*Oof.* I know that face." It's one of the new group that have spoken, a guy about my age, wearing a T-shirt with my book cover on it. "Have you bought the ring yet? I'm a jeweler, so I can get you a killer deal."

Goddamn, the universe really is awesome.

I smile up at him as I take his book. "Where do you work?"

To Do: ☆

Find a realtor for GG

Meeting with accountant

Find an accountant

Exact revenge on Caleb

Clean literally everything

Fix literally everything

Talk to HIM

New Vacuum

Rip up stained carpet in lobby+snackbar

Replace those long lightbulbs in the ceiling

Find out which games in arcade don't work

Fix roof leak

Reconnect security system (at some point)

Find a therapist   First appointment 7/8 @ 2:30

Figure out why my car is making that clanky noise

New bathroom light fixture

Research competitor pricing

Complete the Google Ads course

Locate source of weird smell in back hallway

Buy tampons!!!!!!!!

Finish new website

Create social media graphics for Laser Speed Dating

Start ads on b-day parties

Get a bikini wax... like now

Train kids on new POS system

Kids paint B-day rooms

Stock arcade games

Stock snack bar

Update business hours

New business bank account (Me +Dar only/registered users)

Paint wheel purple/green

Job posting!

EPILOGUE

SAVVY

EIGHTEEN MONTHS LATER

THERE'S a woman in the chair beside mine, her blonde head poking out from behind a book. I can't help but smile because it's one of *my husband's*.

When she looks away for a moment in search of her smoothie, I recognize her as someone I've seen around the resort a few times. She's a few years younger than me, but her husband—who might be a living embodiment of the term "silver fox"—has to be Dar's age.

Things must be going for them well, though, because her hand is resting on a baby bump and she has that happy, relaxed glow of a woman on vacation with the love of her life. I know it well, because it's the same one I saw when I looked in the mirror when we first arrived here.

"Hi." I smile at her as I settle back in my seat.

She looks around, eyebrows lifting in surprise that I'm looking at her, and I feel the usual pinch of self-consciousness that I'm bothering someone.

"Hi." She offers a shy smile back. "I like your hair."

"Oh!" I touch the tips, which I dyed a light, romantic pink

for the wedding. "Thanks! I did the hot-pink thing for years, but it was time for a change."

She sets the book down, and my heart lifts.

"My sister keeps telling me I should go brunette for a while so we look more alike."

I stare at her, considering. "Nah, don't do it. You're so pretty, you don't need to change anything."

Her cheeks flush. "You sound like my husband." She's so cute. I love her. "I'm Savvy, by the way."

"Isobel."

"How long are you here for?"

Her expression goes dreamy. "Still another eight days. You?" "Same! We're from upstate New York."

"Washington, D.C. I grew up in Manhattan, though, and we're up there all the time because Judah's son and my sister live there."

"No way! Such a small world." I'm smiling like a lunatic, pleased with myself for being social. "Also, it's awesome that they both live there. It must make visiting so easy!"

Her flush deepens. "Well, they live there *together*. They're married." She married her sister's father-in-law? Oh, hell yeah, girl. If anything,

I'm impressed. From the way she says it, though—a little defensive—I'm guessing she's used to people making judgements about that.

My cheeks ache from beaming so big. "My husband was best friends with my late father, so I've known him my whole life. Do you think that's better or worse than how you guys met?"

"Wait, seriously?" She's smiling now, and I can sense she's letting down whatever guard went up when I started talking to her.

I nod, and we've both fallen into peals of laughter at the ridiculousness of this chance encounter when the tall, silver-haired man I recognize as Isobel's husband appears. He takes the lounge chair beside hers, looking between us with bemused interest.

"Sorry, honey," Isobel says when the last of our laughs have finally faded away, and she beams at him. "This is my new friend, Savvy. Savvy, this is my husband, Judah."

"No apology necessary." He smiles at me warmly, passing a fresh smoothie to his wife. "Nice to meet you, Savvy. I think I was just speaking to your husband at the bar."

I grin, because I still get a thrill every time I hear that—*my husband*. It's the best. "Tall? Dark hair? Likely scowling? Probably complaining about the sun or sand? Possibly both?"

"Ah." Judah chuckles. "Yes, I believe that's him."

Right on cue, Darwin appears beside my chair, looking unbelievably hot dressed in only a pair of black swim trunks and a loose, unbuttoned cotton shirt. He's holding a ridiculous coconut cocktail with a mini umbrella and fruit sticking out of it, as I requested, and doesn't even look put upon as he hands it to me.

My heart flutters. I love this grump so much.

"Dar, this is Isobel, and her husband, Judah." I gesture to my new friend.

"Hello," he offers obligingly, sitting down beside me and leaning over to kiss my temple.

Isobel squints at him. "You look *super* familiar. Have we met before?"

"I don't believe so."

I laugh, curling closer to my husband, my chest filling with pride. "He wrote the book you're reading."

Isobel's mouth pops open in disbelief. She flips it over, gazing down at the scowling headshot on the back of the paperback cover, up to Dar, then back to the picture.

Judah recovers first, and grins. "Great to meet you. I've read the whole series, but this is Issy's first time. Big fan of your work. I'm excited for the show."

"Thank you," says Dar graciously. He's been making more

of an effort to connect with his readers, attending conventions and book signings semi- regularly now, but I know he's still not used to being recognized.

"Isobel, I booked pedicures for Dar and I in the morning, but he objected to that plan." I shoot him a playful scowl. "Do you want to come with me instead? No pressure, I know you guys are here to spend time together."

Isobel is glowing, though, and a quick glance at her husband (who looks beyond pleased his wife has made a new friend) seems to quell any of her reservations about abandoning him for a few hours.

"Yes. I would love that," she agrees. "Should we exchange numbers?"

We do, then chatter about our plans for our vacations, what we do at home, and our hobbies. Our husbands fall into quiet conversation off to the side, and by the time Isobel says they have to get going for a dinner reservation, we've made plans to have a double lunch date after our spa treatments tomorrow.

"Text me in the morning! We can get baby-safe drinks before our appointment!" I call after her as they leave, and my heart is so full.

"You like her," Dar observes, and he nudges me forward so he can slide behind me.

I sigh happily and settle back against his warm chest, sipping my drink. "I've kind of avoided making new friends for a while. Raven says I'm obsessed with her."

His hand roams over my bare stomach, settling below my belly button, and I know what's on his mind. "Do you think it's already happened?" he asks in my ear, voice thick with longing.

I giggle, pushing my fingers through his. "If it hasn't, it's not for lack of effort. You're obsessed."

He really is. Since we decided to start trying, the man has been reading every book about conception, pregnancy, and parenting he can get his hands on. My proposal to get drunk and have sex on the living room floor was *not* appreciated (though we did it anyway).

I probably should have known it would be like this. When my husband puts his mind to something, there's no stopping him.

Dar's warm breath ghosts over my ear, raising goose-bumps over my arms that are at odds with the sticky, tropical air. "Do you know what I was thinking about a moment ago?"

I shake my head, admiring the matching wedding bands on our fingers as I sip my drink. "If it's my current level of cervical mucus, I'm leaving you."

He ignores me. "The plug in your tight ass. How does it feel, little tornado?"

Oh. Right. I should have guessed that's where he was going with this.

Smirking, I shift a little, enjoying the sensation. "Full," I admit. "It's bigger than I'm used to."

"Not as big as I am." I can't see him, but I know exactly which smug, satisfied smirk he's wearing right now.

My eyelids flutter. "Are you going to fuck my ass tonight, husband?" It's an intimidating prospect, but I'm up for a challenge.

To my disappointment, Dar chuckles. "No, wife. Until I knock you up, the only place my cum is going is your pussy. I had something else in mind. No rush, though. Enjoy your drink."

I take a long sip, slurping noisily, and his chest shakes with laughter. Setting the coconut on the table beside the lounger, I lean over so I can meet my Dar's eyes. "Can we go back to the bungalow now?"

It doesn't take much convincing, and soon we're walking hand in hand through the resort, the late-afternoon tropical sun on our backs.

Despite saying Dar would never pull off something like the signing at Galactic Guild again, this entire trip was a surprise. He very sneakily told me I'd need to get a passport about six months ago so I could accompany him to a conference in Montreal. He coordinated with Marley, who is now my assistant manager while she goes to community college, and I didn't realize anything was afoot until he handed me my ticket in line for security at the airport.

I arrived in Bora Bora with a suitcase full of jeans and sweatshirts, so our first stop was an expensive little boutique, where my new husband was happy to sit back and give his opinions on my new selection of floaty cotton sundresses and tiny bikinis.

My hand tightens in his as we step onto the dock that leads to a big loop of private, over-water bungalows, ours among them. "When did you decide to do this? I never asked."

Dar hums, his eyes on the ocean. "Right after we got engaged. It occurred to me we've never had an extended period to just enjoy each other's company, uninterrupted. There's always so much going on."

This guy. "You're very romantic, for a science-fiction author. Tell me, Mr. Wilder, will there be any *open door* scenes in your next book? As your number one fan, I can tell you those fade-to-black moments were *very* frustrating."

"I bet they were." He smirks, and as we turn onto the little pathway toward our bungalow, a weight drops into my lower belly.

If sex with Dar was incredible in the beginning of our relationship, it's leveled up since we got married, and I'm addicted. Now, with the baby- making efforts… the situation has officially gotten out of hand. Our first two days here, we didn't even leave the bedroom.

Neither of us speak as the door closes behind us, and a sly glance over my shoulder confirms Dar is on the same page.

"Bed," he grunts, eyes roaming over my body, which has gotten tanner in the few days since we've emerged from our sex bubble. I haven't been bothering with actual clothing unless we're going out to eat, and the pale-pink bikini that matches my hair now feels too tight.

Giggling, I almost trip over myself as I book it through the living area to our bedroom, which was freshened up while we were out. The big windows are open, and the ocean breeze is making the gauzy white canopy over the massive bed flutter.

"I still can't believe you did this for me." I sigh, my fingers moving under the bands of my bathing suit without turning. He's there. The weight of his gaze makes heat prickle restlessly under my skin as I let my top fall, the soft brush of the fabric lost in the sound of the waves lapping against the bungalow's supports. My bottoms go next, and I bend over to guide them down my legs, making sure he can see the pink, heart-shaped jewel resting between my cheeks.

The sex shop located right across the road from the boutique where we bought all my vacation clothes was a *very* lucky find.

I gasp when a pair of large, warm hands settle on my bare waist, and Dar's lips brush over the curve of my neck to nip at my ear. "I would do anything for you."

My breath catches. "Dar…"

"Get on your knees for me, baby. I need your mouth."

God, I love it when he talks to me like this. There's no pretending that the low, authoritative order doesn't make my pulse spike and my breasts heavy. Turning in his arms, I pause only to push the cotton shirt off his shoulders before dropping to my knees.

Dar is already hard, the long ridge of his erection tenting his trunks, and my mouth waters as I pull them down, freeing his cock. Leaning forward, I drag my tongue along the underside of his shaft, tasting the ocean on his skin.

I keep my pace slow and worshipful, kissing and licking

every inch before I finally lift my eyes to meet his and take him fully in my mouth. His tip bumps the back of my throat, but I keep going, forcing myself to relax as I take more of him than I ever have before.

The temporary discomfort is worth it for the way Dar is shaking, a low stream of praise and curses coming from his lips. I love doing this to him, reducing my bigger, stronger, older husband to a shuddering mess. It might seem counter-intuitive, but I never feel more powerful than when he's using me for his pleasure.

When my nose brushes the dark, wiry hair at the base of his cock, he pulls me off. "Get on the bed," he grits out as he stares down at me, chest heaving. "Ass in the air."

I'm panting too as I hurry to do as he says, crawling onto the edge of the mattress and spreading my thighs.

"So eager, baby. I wish you could see how you look right now," Dar murmurs behind me, his hands caressing my behind. I moan quietly, squirming as he presses on the end of the plug. "Dripping wet from sucking my cock and having your cute little ass stretched."

Without warning, three fingers plunge into my pussy. The wet, sloppy noises that come from him guiding them in and out of my body make my face burn. I'm still tender from the sheer quantity (and quality) of sex we've been having, but I think I might die if he doesn't fuck me.

"That's my girl," Dar coos, and the head of his cock brushes the backs of my thighs, smearing pre-cum over the sensitive skin. "So greedy. Are you going to let me stuff both your holes full?"

Holy crap.

I'm shaking with need now and barely aware of what I'm saying. It must be affirmative, though, because I absolutely do want that. I'm not a total stranger to anal play, but we've never done this before. When Dar's fingers pull free from my pussy, a nervous thrill settles in my core.

He isn't fucking around. Seconds later, the head of my husband's thick cock is pressing against my entrance.

"That's it." Dar's praise is strained as he eases forward.

It's… a lot. The pressure is intense. I can feel the ridge of the plug pressing against his cock, and, judging by the way his hands tighten on my hips, Dar feels it too.

"Shit," I whimper, arching my back to give him more space. The rest of his length slides in, leaving me impossibly full.

Dar doesn't move, and when I rock against him, his hands tighten, forcing me to be still. "You feel incredible, baby. Tighter than my fucking fist—shit. Hold still or I'm going to fill you after one pump."

My tongue darts out to wet my lips. "It's so full."

"I know. I can feel it." He begins to move, easing back a few inches, then forward in slow, measured thrusts. "Such a good girl, letting me stuff your little holes. I bet you'd take more if I asked you to."

I let out a hysterical little giggle, wetness spreading to my inner thighs. "That's probably not possible."

I squeak when a long finger slides into my pussy alongside his cock.

It's just for a second, and his silent laugh rumbles through both of us as he pulls it back, not losing the slow rhythm he's fucking me with. Seconds later, that finger is being pushed into my mouth. "Suck me clean, then you're going to get it rough."

He isn't kidding. No sooner have my lips fallen open again than his thrusts become harsh. My hands scrabble helplessly at the mattress as the overload of sensations makes me almost dizzy. It seems unbelievable that I could come like this, but Dar's cock is everywhere, and it's not long before my legs are shaking.

"I'm gonna come," I slur. "*Please*, I need, I need—" He knows what I need.

The rough pinch to my clit is all it takes to send me over the edge. I'm still shaking, reeling from the intensity of my orgasm, when Dar's pace begins to falter.

"Tell me where you want my cum," he demands, clutching my hips so hard that there will probably be bruises.

Oh fuck, that's so hot.

I moan. "Come inside me, *please*, Dar. I need it deep!"

"Yeah?" Our skin slaps together, and the knot of pleasure hasn't fully unwound before it starts to tighten again, one orgasm rolling into the next. "You're not on birth control, baby. Do you want it anyway? Do you want me to get you pregnant?"

I come again, so hard that if it weren't his hands holding me up, I would have fallen flat on the mattress.

He slaps my ass. "Tell me."

"Get me pregnant, please, Dar."

There's a rough curse, and a few frantic pumps later, he stills, pressing deep. The warm, wet lash of his cum coats my inner walls, filling me in more ways than one.

I peek over my shoulder, and my stomach flips at the sight of Dar's expression. He's staring at the place where we're still connected, jaw slack from the pleasure he's taken from my body and the intimacy of this moment.

Our eyes meet, and a slow, lazy smile curls my lips.

He shakes his head, like he's just as lost for words as I am, and pulls out. I feel his release and my own dripping out after him, but long fingers gather it up, pushing every drop back in. "Are you okay?" he finally asks as he eases the plug out and lets it fall to the floor.

My face still pressed against the sheets, I nod, humming. Dar crawls over me and gathers me close, kissing the crown of my hair. "I love you," I mumble, my eyes fluttering shut as I play absently with the coarse hairs of his beard.

Another kiss, this time to my temple. "I love you back." His voice is distant, though, distracted.

I crack one eye back open. "Are you okay?"

His answering smile is warm and relaxed. "I'm better than okay. I'm… I didn't know it was possible. To be this happy every day."

My heart swells. "Well, we are on vacation," I remind him, nodding toward the crystal-clear ocean beyond the window of the bedroom. "It's pretty hard to be upset about anything when we're here."

"Where we are has nothing to do with it, Savvy." As he stares down at me, there's something more than love in his dark eyes. "*You're* it."

———

Thank you so much for reading! If you enjoyed this story, please take the time to leave a rating or review. It is such an enormous help for indie authors like myself, and I genuinely love hearing people's thoughts on my work!

- Cleo

AFTERWORD

Want to see if Savvy gets her sparkly dress for the premier of Dar's show? Download a free bonus epilogue here!

If you'd like to read Isobel and Judah's forbidden love story, Out of Sight is available now. Keep reading for an excerpt!

OUT OF SIGHT TEASER

"Going on vacation?"

I blink, tearing my eyes from my computer screen to find the old woman in the seat beside mine gazing at me expectantly.

"Um. No. I'm going to my sister's wedding." I shut my laptop, giving her the same pained, obligatory smile I usually reserve for the girl in my chem class who licks her fingers before turning the pages of our *shared* lab packet. Not that it matters. I could probably bare my teeth and growl at this woman, and it wouldn't put her off. We've been on this plane for three hours, and she's tried to make conversation with me at least six times, apparently mistaking my utter lack of interest for shyness.

Isn't there a rule in the airplane safety pamphlet about leaving the stranger next to you alone, or is that just common courtesy?

The woman—whom I mentally dubbed "Old Bat" before the plane had even taken off—lights up, clasping her hands to her chest like I told her Evie cured an incurable disease. Joke's

on her, though. Evie isn't scheduled to cure pediatric pleu-
ropulmonary blastoma for another four years. Considering
my sister still hasn't deviated from the life plan she finalized
at age fourteen, I'd hold her to that. "How *exciting*! A destina-
tion wedding? Are you the Maid of Honor?"

Holy hell. I feel like I'm staring into an intellectual black
hole.

"Yup." I'm not, nor did I expect to be, but Old Bat doesn't
need to know that. My sister is six years older than I am. By
the time I was old enough to speak in full sentences, she was
off to boarding school. We never had those formative years of
bickering and bonding, and now the only thing we have in
common is our eye color and the undying urge to please our
parents. This trip, a full week in Bora Bora for her wedding,
will be the most time I've spent with any of my family
members in years.

I've met my future brother-in-law, Reuben, only once, and
that was at my grandmother's Passover seder last year. We
didn't speak much but, from what I could tell, he seemed like
exactly the kind of guy Evie would always end up with—
intelligent and easygoing enough to balance out her type-A
neurosis. They met on the very first day of medical school,
but didn't start dating until they were placed into the same
pediatric oncology residency, falling in love over kids with
cancer and after-work espresso martinis.

Old Bat beams. "Oh, I was the maid of honor for my sister.
She got married in Florida the year... *oh.* When was it? Well,
anyway, they divorced only a few years later because—"

Alright, I'm out.

My noise-canceling headphones died just as I was getting
on the plane, but Old Bat doesn't know that. Not bothering to
make up an excuse, I pull them out of my bag and snap them
on while she's halfway through the word "potpourri." I can
see her offended pout in the corner of my eye, but I stare
determinedly down at my phone, aimlessly scrolling until

she's safely turned away to talk to the poor flight attendant. Reflexively, I reopen my laptop, hitting refresh on my email for the third time in the last fifteen minutes.

Why hasn't it come yet?

Everything I've worked for, the parties I didn't go to, and the countless late nights in the library, have all come down to one email.

Going to Weston Medical School is what the Bradley family *does*. My great-grandfather started the tradition before going on to become one of the founding fathers of cardiothoracic surgery. My grandfather followed in his footsteps, developing a procedure that has saved thousands of lives. Then my father, who met and later married my equally brilliant mother there, undoubtedly hoping to create an elite, hybrid generation of Doctor Bradleys to conquer the world one medical innovation at a time.

It half worked.

I know I'm not an idiot, but as I head into the final semester of my undergraduate education, it seems pretty ridiculous to pretend I'm a match for my sister. Evie graduated a year early with honors, perfect test scores, a letter of recommendation from the dean, and a handful of prestigious internships under her belt. All with a flawless manicure, a pack of loyal girlfriends, and an apartment that could have been on the cover of *Organized Living*.

I am graduating a year late because of that semester off. I've been advised—ordered—never to mention a non-existent social life and an academic record that's good but not exceptional.

Also, her boobs are, like, twice the size of mine. Talk about some bullshit.

Something in my chest knots painfully, and I force myself to take a long, slow breath. It's going to be fine. I'm being ridiculous. I might not be as utterly, incomprehensibly perfect as Evie, but that doesn't mean I won't get in. I've worked hard, I have recommendations from my professors, and I've been volunteering for over two years. If all that doesn't seal the deal, I'm not too proud to rely on the three generations of Weston alumni who share my last name for some of those sweet nepotism points.

"Good afternoon, passengers. The captain has turned on the fasten seatbelt sign —"

The clouds clear away as the plane drops lower, and now I can see a beautiful island settled atop the crystal-clear ocean beyond the wing of the plane. My parents went all out, buying out half of a boutique Bora Bora resort for Evie and Reuben's wedding—the very same one that they were married at nearly thirty years ago.

The immediate families of the bride and groom will be arriving today, five full days early, and we'll be joined by the rest of the guests the night before the wedding. Evie wanted my parents to get to know Reuben's by doing what she does best: organizing. She emailed everyone a five-page, color-coded schedule, which includes helpful reminders to regularly re-apply sunscreen and hydrate. Our parents and I will be subjected to five full days of forced bonding activities and wedding organizing with these strangers before my sister deems us sufficiently integrated and we're permitted to return to our separate corners of the country.

Beneath me, the plane jerks, and I grip my armrests so hard that my knuckles turn white, prompting an alarmed look from Old Bat.

I know it's not normal to feel this way before seeing your family, and that there's probably a therapist out there who will someday make a lot of money off me, but normally I can handle it. I was counting on having a med-school acceptance to lessen their general disappointment in me, though, and my Weston-free inbox has notched my anxiety up to a near-critical level.

They're going to ask about it, *of course*, they're going to ask about it, and I feel sick just thinking about the pursed lips and quiet sighs I'll get when I tell them, *"No, I haven't heard yet."* They haven't said it out loud, but I can't quite manage to dismiss the gnawing suspicion that I've already been sort of… written off.

Having high-powered surgeons as parents tends to translate into a certain level of emotional neglect. I'm used to that, but it's been impossible not to form parallels between those months before Evie applied to medical school and when I did. They were so excited for her. My mother was constantly calling to discuss application essay questions and which apartment buildings they ought to look at, while my father conveniently invited an old friend who works in the admissions office to dinner.

There'd been none of that for me. Is it because they think I don't have a chance of getting in, or—

No. I shove the thought aside.

They've been busy, that's all. Evie's wedding is coming up, my mother is up for that big award, and my father's practice partner retired earlier than planned, so his caseload has been crazy. Those are all perfectly valid reasons for them not calling me every hour to talk about Weston. I'm being selfish. This is Evie's wedding week and, no matter how shitty our parents make me feel, I refuse to make it even a little bit about me.

I keep my eyes on the runway as the plane makes its final descent, palm trees and crystalline waters flashing by until we land with a jerk, bumping and skidding toward a small airport with only half a dozen planes outside.

The moment the flight attendants open the doors, a wall of humidity and the scent of the nearby ocean hit me like a wall. Old Bat takes her time gathering up her free copy of *Air Times Magazine*, three unopened bags of peanuts, and a fuzzy purple neck pillow before finally rising and allowing me to escape the suddenly unbearable, claustrophobic plane onto the hot tarmac.

It's nearly noon, and the sun is high. So, by the time I get my bags from the luggage claim and drag them out to the line of hotel shuttles and taxis, my t-shirt is clinging to my back, and I'm panting. A quick glance at myself in my phone's camera is enough to confirm I look exactly as shitty as I knew I would after spending fifteen hours getting on and off planes, sitting next to overly chatty old ladies, and eating fistfuls of flavorless snacks in between bouts of uncomfortable sleep.

In other words, *really* shitty.

As far as I know, no one in our family or Reuben's will be arriving until later this afternoon. With any luck, I should be able to escape to my hotel room unnoticed and clean up before dinner tonight—the first event on Evie's schedule.

I want to collapse in relief when I finally find a white shuttle van adorned with the logo of the Regency Sun Resort & Spa, the driver leaning against it with a cigarette between his fingers. He throws it away as I approach, giving my body an appreciative look as he welcomes me to Bora Bora in heavily accented English. "You are not the bride, no?" he asks as I climb up into the van.

He's objectively attractive, maybe a year or two older than me with floppy brown hair and golden-brown skin; the perfect vacation fling, if you're into that sort of thing. I'm positive I'm not the only pretty foreigner he's made eyes at, nor will I be the last. I almost wish I could. Having someone to take my mind off Weston and the family stress would be great, but, unfortunately, I've learned the hard way that rationalizing someone's attractiveness isn't actually going to make me attracted to them.

"No, I'm not the bride," I assure him quietly, settling back in my seat and brushing the sticky strands of hair out of my face. The van is thankfully air-conditioned, but the flirty driver makes no move to shut the door.

"We have another guest arriving," he tells me over his shoulder just as another exhausted-looking traveler approaches, dragging a suitcase with a garment bag slung over his arm and dressed in wrinkled clothes.

I still, my chest suddenly tight.

The newcomer must be in his mid-forties, but he's in better shape than the driver, who is half his age. Broad-shouldered and tall, he towers over the travelers walking past him on the sidewalk, checking the logo on the van from behind thick-framed black glasses. He looks like a silver-haired Clark Kent, and I realize with a jolt I've been pressing my thighs together as heat pools low in my belly.

Um. What?

"Regency Sun?" confirms the driver, glancing over his shoulder at me with a sly little smile, like we're in on a secret.

"That's right," the newcomer says, his voice low and weary. "How far are we from the resort?"

"Oh, about fifteen minutes, very easy drive," the driver informs him, taking the man's luggage around to the back.

I watch, my lungs burning with a breath I can't quite manage to exhale, as the stranger casts a long, lasting look over his shoulder like he's looking for someone. Shaking his head slightly, he turns and moves to the van's open door, making to step up. When our eyes meet, however, he stops dead, staring at me.

There might be some staring back. Because, holy shit, he's hot. Really hot. Even sticky with sweat and clearly just as ruffled from sitting on an airplane as I am. My cheeks warm. Oh god, I look so bad right now. But he's still looking at me; not my body, but straight into my eyes.

A metallic thud makes both of us jump, and the stranger's eyes finally move from mine to the van floor, where his phone has fallen from his hand and is lying face down on the metal frame around the door. Cursing quietly, he picks it up, wincing at the spiderweb of cracks running through the screen.

Oops.

"Sir?" The driver is back, and the newcomer shoves the device in his pocket before stepping up inside. This van has four rows of seats, but he takes the one across the aisle from me.

It feels like my whole body is suddenly attached to a live wire. My entire consciousness is focused on the stranger sitting just a few feet away from me, and my heart is suddenly hammering frantically against my ribcage. This has *never* happened to me. Ever. I have several ex-boyfriends who could attest to my complete disinterest in them.

I always rolled my eyes at the girls in school who became gooey, fluttery messes when the right boy smiled their way, but I'm feeling pretty gooey and fluttery right now.

"Where are you coming from?"

I look around so quickly that a muscle in my neck spasms painfully. "Oh!" I rub it, wincing. His voice is *great*, low, and just a little gravely. "Sorry. I've clearly been sitting on a plane for too long. Um, I'm here from Chicago, but I flew through Tahiti. You?"

He grins sheepishly, like I've caught him in the act. "Washington D.C. But I, ah, was on the same connecting flight. I noticed you."

Oh. Okay, wow. I hope he didn't hear me stonewall Old Bat when she asked me the same question he just did.

The front door slams as the driver climbs in, turning to give me a crooked smile that is obviously designed to be charming. "We'll be at the resort in no time," he tells me smoothly, completely ignoring his other passenger. "Please let me know if you need anything to improve your stay, Miss..." He trails off, waiting for me to give my name.

I grimace, but before I can make something up, my

stranger does. "Mrs," he informs the driver nonchalantly, so casually he might have been reporting the weather conditions. Without hesitation, he reaches across the aisle to weave his fingers through my hand where it's resting in my lap. "We're here for our anniversary."

The driver's lips pinch like he doesn't quite believe him, but thankfully turns back around and directs his attention to the road, fiddling with the radio as we pull into airport traffic.

My stranger doesn't release my hand, though. "Should I hold your hand a while longer, just to be safe?" he asks under his breath, the corner of his lips lifting in a mischievous smile. There's something about him that screams *professional*, like he spends his days in a suit and knows how to create one hell of a spreadsheet, but when he smiles….

Butterflies. Actual butterflies erupt inside me. Holy hell, I'm twenty-three years old. It's a little late for a first crush.

"I—Yes. Yes, please." I can't believe this is happening. It's like I've stumbled out of a depressing black-and-white indie movie into a rom-com meet cute. Or I would, if it weren't for the fact he's at least twenty years older than me, and I'm pretty much the definition of emotionally unavailable. I can flirt with him, though, can't I? "So, our anniversary, huh? How many years? In case he asks, of course."

"*Of course,*" my stranger agrees solemnly, his eyes sparkling behind his glasses. "Two years, I think."

I hum thoughtfully, loving the feeling of his skin against mine and how his thumb drags slowly over the side of my hand, almost unconsciously. "Why two?"

His low chuckle goes right through me, spreading warmth that has nothing to do with the tropical climate. "We arrived at the shuttle separately, didn't we? It would take at least two years for me to be able to let you out of my sight. Do you know what? No. Three. Definitely three."

Cue exponential increase of gooey and fluttery feelings.

Is this actually happening? This isn't me. I'm awkward, prickly, and generally unsociable. My own family doesn't like spending time with me, and I've been operating under the assumption that if the people genetically obligated to like me don't, why would anyone else? I don't ever go out of my way to talk to people, but there's something in how this guy looks at me that makes all those usual worries disappear.

"Don't you think you should learn my name before signing up for that kind of commitment?"

His answering bark of laughter makes my heart feel full. "No." He shakes his head, still grinning. "Tell me anyway. It might be useful."

"Isobel."

His smile grows bigger. "Judah."

From the front seat, the driver has his eyes on me in the rearview mirror as he calls back, "How long have you been married?"

He looks back at the road when Judah and I respond in unison, "Three years!"

ABOUT THE AUTHOR

Cleo White's affinity for all things dark, dramatic, and hopelessly romantic began the day she was born, which happened to be in the middle of a record-breaking snowstorm on Valentine's Day. Her love of literature came soon after, and she spent the better part of her childhood with both a book and a notebook full of unfinished stories in hand. Later in life, she found a love of writing spicy books with complicated characters and dysfunctional family drama. Cleo currently lives in Vermont with her husband and two daughters. When not writing, she can be found hiking, gardening, painting, and consuming excessive quantities of caffeine.

To stay up to date with upcoming releases and receive exclusive bonus content, subscribe to my newsletter at www.authorcleowhite.com

ALSO BY CLEO WHITE

In the mood for more forbidden insta-love, age-gap, spicy goodness? Check out Cleo's other books!

Out of Sight

In Pieces

Age of Shade

You're It

The Storm

Silver Fox A-Listers Series

Actor

Artist

Rocker